"I hope you don't mind, but I took a shower."

His comment forced her to turn and acknowledge him, but the moment she laid eyes on his damp and masculine form, she froze.

Sweet mercy. He was wearing his shorts, thankfully, but his hair was wet, and he was still shirtless. He walked toward her—barefoot, she assumed, because she couldn't take her eyes off the muscles rippling in his chest long enough to look. The hair on his upper body formed a soft V that angled down below his waistband.

"Maxine?"

She couldn't answer. She was too mesmerized by his ripped hard abdomen.

"Maxine?" he said again, and she had to drag her eyes upward. He stepped closer, and she leaned back against the kitchen counter to steady her shaky legs.

"Huh?" she managed to get out.

Cooper was now only inches away. He lifted his hand to her face, his fingers skimming her cheek and setting her skin on fire. "If you don't stop looking at me like that, I'm not going to be able to control myself anymore."

She didn't want him to control himself. And she was sure as heck tired of controlling herself. So she raised her lips in invitation.

And that was all it took.

W9-CFK-267

**Sugar Falls, Idaho:
Your destination for true love!**

Dear Reader,

Coming up with ideas for stories is a little like making Maxine Walker's famous Sugar Falls Cookie recipe. I take a bit of life experience and blend in some personal observations before adding my own imagination to the mix. In *A Marine for His Mom*, there are several ingredients that I blended to make this romance come together.

During law school, I interned at the Office of the Staff Judge Advocate and developed a better understanding and respect for the men and women who serve in our military. And given my history in law enforcement, having a military cop as the hero was a perfect start. I've also been known to shake a few pom-poms in my day and, like the heroine, I have several close girlfriends from college with whom I group text constantly. But the character I relate to most in this book is the young matchmaker determined to find the perfect guy for his single mother. I mean, come on... What kid from a divorced home wouldn't love the opportunity to set up one of their parents?

Like Hunter Walker, I met my future stepdad when I was ten years old. We bonded over our shared dislike of onions in our meatloaf—or any other meal. And while I can't take credit for setting them up, I couldn't have picked a better match for my mom.

For more information on my pantry of life experiences, visit my website at christyjeffries.com, or chat with me on Twitter at @ChristyJeffries. You can also find me on Facebook and Instagram. I'd love to hear from you! And don't miss *Waking Up Wed*, the next book in my Sugar Falls, Idaho miniseries, coming in February 2016!

Enjoy,

Christy Jeffries

A Marine
for His Mom

Christy Jeffries

HARLEQUIN® SPECIAL EDITION®

Recycling programs
for this product may
not exist in your area.

ISBN-13: 978-0-373-65936-4

A Marine for His Mom

Printed in U.S.A.

Christy Jeffries graduated from the University of California, Irvine, with a degree in criminology and received her Juris Doctor from California Western School of Law. But drafting court documents and working in law enforcement was merely an apprenticeship for her current career in the dynamic field of mommyhood and romance writing. She lives in Southern California with her patient husband, two energetic sons and one sassy grandmother. Follow her online at christyjeffries.com.

To the wise and determined bestselling author, Judy Duarte. When my English teacher told you that I didn't like to read, you handed me a Danielle Steel book and said, "Try reading a romance novel." And when I struggled with the decision to leave a rewarding career to become a stay-at-home mom, you signed me up for a workshop and said, "Try writing a romance novel."

It takes a strong woman to guide an even stronger-willed daughter. But doing it with such grace, diplomacy and unconventional orchestration takes extreme love and dedication.

I love you, Mom.

Prologue

September 4

Dear Soldier,
My name is Hunter Walker. I'm a fifth grader in Miss Gregson's class. I live in Sugar Falls, Idaho, which is the most boringest town you can think of. I love football and baseball, even though my mom won't let me play. Gram says my dad was the best football player to ever come out of Sugar Falls, but he died when I was a baby and before he made the pros. Since I'm not allowed to play, I never have anything to do when my mom is busy working or with her friends.

My mom is nice but she is way to into her girl stuff. She has a cool bakery that's famous for cookies and her friends are always trying to find stuff for me to do. Aunt Mia had me in yoga, but I got sick of being the only boy. Aunt Kylie wanted to enter me in one of her glitz pageants last year, but when I saw the glittery pink bow tie, I said no way. Gram tries to talk mom into letting me play football, but my mom says it'll never happen. Mom says Gram is to pushy and needs to learn to back off. I think Gram is fine except when she buys me clothes that make me feel like a big fat loser. I never get to do any cool boy things. Even though I don't remember him, I sometimes miss my dad. It would be nice to talk to a guy once in awhile. I don't really have anything in common with the other boys in my class and they make fun of me a lot.

I put in a picture of me so you would know who your writing to. Can you send me a picture of you? Maybe one of you on an M1A1 tank or in a fighter plane. Any plane or Huey would be cool, but Jake Marconi says his uncle flies a Harrier jet and I saw one when I looked it up online. I think Jake is lying because I met his uncle at Jake's 8th birthday party and he didn't look like a fighter pilot. Can you be a fighter pilot when your 18? Do they have fighter pilots in the coast guard?

Its ok if your not a fighter pilot. I'll still write you back. But you are a man right? I don't want to have to write to any girls cause I have to be around them enough already. Do you like baseball? Or UFC? I'm not allowed to watch UFC, but my mom lets me watch baseball. The Colorado Rockies are my favorite team and I know every stat about them for the last three years. Anyway, I hope your a boy and that you like baseball and that you write me back.
Sincerely,
Hunter Walker

Chapter One

Gunnery Sergeant Matthew Cooper closed his eyes and clenched the armrests as his plane touched down onto the tarmac in Boise. No matter how many times he'd flown to obscure places around the world, he never got used to the steady decline and the rough bounce of the landing. But this time, he felt as if his entire future was skidding toward the edge of the runway.

A couple of months ago, when he'd stormed out of his commanding officer's makeshift headquarters with Hunter Walker's letter crumpled in his hand, he'd been mad as hell. He'd been even *more* pissed off at Dr. Gregson for suggesting he participate in the ridiculous pen pal program and pairing him up with some goofy kid in Nowheresville, Idaho.

As the seat belt light dinged off, Cooper remembered thinking that a Marine Corps base in Afghanistan wasn't any place for him to be playing nanny-by-mail to some ten-year-old kid with an overprotective mom and no friends. It wasn't as if Cooper had been some lonely nineteen-year-old infantry grunt who needed a morale boost. He'd been a provost sergeant who'd held some of the deadliest Taliban leaders in custody in the base brig. Before that, he'd been stationed as an MP at bases all over the world. He'd broken up bar fights, investigated assaults and murder, and even gone undercover with NCIS on a few occasions. He had no business being some kid's babysitter or even worse, male role model.

But now that Cooper's tour of duty, and possibly his entire military career, was at a sudden end thanks to a random suicide bomber, that same kid and the bond they'd established over emails and letters was the only glimpse of brightness in his dark, lonely future.

As the center aisle of the aircraft filled up with people trying to reclaim their belongings from the overhead bins, Cooper fiddled with his seat belt and longed to stand and stretch out his legs. But his knee was barely being held together with pins and screws, and he would have to wait for the rest of the passengers to disembark the plane before some airline personnel would load him up on a wheelchair and push his useless body out to the baggage claim area.

He hated being weak and was questioning his earlier decision to allow Hunter to see him like this the first time they met. He ached with stiffness, and he was completely exhausted. He'd been traveling on a commercial airline for well over thirty hours now, with layovers in both Tokyo and San Francisco. He'd taken a Vicodin in the Frisco airport an hour before he boarded the last leg of his flight, and now he wondered whether he was in any shape to meet his young pen pal face-to-face.

Or to allow the kid's mom to drive him to the Shadowview Military Hospital outside of Boise.

Crap. How had he let Hunter talk him into that? Sure, he and the chatty fifth grader had built up quite the steady stream of correspondence when he'd been stationed in Afghanistan, and then later, as he'd been recuperating at the closest base hospital. And although he wasn't what most people would consider a believer in divine intervention, Cooper had to question the alignment of fate when the doctors in Okinawa told him that the two best options he had to recover the use of his leg would be an intense orthopedic surgery at either Walter Reed Medical Center in Maryland or the Shadowview Military Hospital outside of Boise.

Cooper's distal femur fracture would need to be repaired and healed before they could even think about a total knee replacement. He was looking at a long recovery time and, while he normally didn't mind his loner lifestyle or the fact that he didn't have any family to speak of, he figured that if he went to Shadowview, he'd at least be close to Hunter.

How pathetic was that?

He tried to comfort himself with the belief that Hunter needed him. The kid didn't have any positive male role models, and while the boy's mom probably loved him, it sounded like Hunter really needed a strong hand to get him in check. What the hell was wrong with the kid's mother? Putting him in yoga classes and forbidding sports? Who does that to a boy? Guessing by her baking job, she was probably just as out of shape as the kid—if not more so—and too busy working to bother with taking care of her son.

It had been a bone of contention between Cooper and his ex-wife, but one thing Cooper had learned early on in the foster care system was that people shouldn't be having kids if they were too busy to raise them.

That old familiar pang cramped inside his left rib cage, and he grabbed his backpack from under the seat just to give himself something to do. He winced as the forward movement added pressure to his leg, but the physical pain was at least better than the emotional pain that he'd almost let get the better of him.

There seemed to be some sort of delay exiting the plane because nobody was moving forward. Cooper pulled the printout of one of his past emails from Hunter from his backpack and read it.

To: matthewcooper@usmc.mil
From: hunterlovestherockies@hotmail.net
Re: Surgery
Date: Jan 3
Wow! I can't believe your actually coming Idaho to have your operation. How long do you have to stay in the hospital? I'll have my mom and my Gram bring me down every week to visit you. Maybe I can hitchhike rides down the mountain too, when my mom is working. Jake Marconi said he hitchhiked once with his cousin and they went all the way to Winnemucca.

Are you real real worried about your knee? I'd be crazy worried if I were you. They should probably award your dog Helix a purple heart or a navy cross or something for going after that bomber and saving your life like that. Will they let you still be a marine if your knee don't heal right?

You can still be my pen pal even if they kick you out and you're not a marine no more. Where will you live when you get out of the hospital?

I went to Hawaii once with Gram. You could live there. Or even better, you could come live HERE. In Sugar Falls. It would be sooooooooooo cool if we could hang out all the time. I'd be the only kid in my class to actually meet his real pen pal. I think I'm the only one now to still be getting letters and emails and stuff. Please please please think about living here after you get done at the hospital. I know I said Sugar Falls was dumb and boring, but it's not really that way if we have each other we can hang out with. We could go fishing and everything.

You could stay with me and my mom. You'll meet her when we pick you up at the airport to take you to the hospital. She'll tell you that it'll be so awesome. Please say yes!

Please.

Hunter

Cooper folded up the paper, and then looked at the standard issue class picture Hunter had sent in his original letter. He almost winced at the chubbiness of the kid's face. The boy's mom needed to get him off the cookies and onto a physical regimen, stat. Cooper may have had it rough growing up in a one-bedroom apartment in the slums of Detroit, but at least he'd been in shape and hadn't taken any crap from the kids on the playground. Of course, taking crap from his stepdad was another thing.

Don't think about the past. Think about the next step. The old adage he'd learned from his drill instructor had helped him to get past his crappy home life and rise up in the ranks. Even after his injury, he'd repeated the mantra dozens of times and knew that no matter how jacked up his leg was, he was a fighter and would get through this.

Once the surgeries were done, the physical therapy would be intense if Cooper wanted to regain full use of his leg. Maybe he could encourage Hunter to do some exercises with him. Heck, maybe Ms. Walker would be willing to get in shape with them.

The past few weeks, he'd found himself wondering

about the boy's mom more frequently. And no, it had nothing to do with the fact that he'd lost his own mom at the age of twelve and had fantasized about what it would be like to have a real home. And loving parents.

So he'd talked to Hunter to make sure that the mother was okay with their pen pal relationship. He'd never written to the woman directly, nor had Hunter ever sent a picture of her, but Cooper had her pegged all the same. As an MP, he could read between the lines.

He didn't want to overstep his boundaries or cause problems for the Walkers. But the woman's world most likely revolved around cookies and not much else. By the time she got around to noticing he was even in her son's life, Cooper would be long gone.

"Mom, can't you make this thing go any faster? Jake Marconi's dad got a new Porsche, and Jake said it can go like a hundred and sixty miles an hour."

Maxine Walker shot a glance across the seat at her impressionable son, yet her mind was focused on how quickly she and Hunter could greet his soldier friend at the airport and make it back up to Sugar Falls before dark. She could care less about Jake Marconi's dad's latest midlife cry for attention. Besides, they'd gotten another couple inches of snow last night, and she didn't like this two-lane stretch of highway down the mountain, even in optimal weather.

"Hunter, explain to me why we have to pick this guy up, again? Doesn't the military provide him transportation to the hospital?"

"I told you. I promised him I'd meet him in person. How would you like to be blown up in a war zone and then fly all the way around the world to some random hospital where you don't know anybody? He's a war hero, Mom. It's our patriotic duty."

Maxine blew a blond curl out of her eye as she finally turned her SUV off the highway and toward the interstate that would take them toward the Boise Airport. She didn't need her ten-year-old son to preach to her about patriotic duties. Maxine had grown up on Uncle Sam's rhetoric. Both of her parents were career Army and had bounced her and her six siblings around from base to base until she finally left for Boise State at eighteen.

"I think you've boosted enough troop morale for all of us these past few months, Hunter. Isn't it enough that I let you keep writing letters to this guy, even though we don't know anything about him?"

"What are you talking about? I know *everything* about Cooper. He's my best friend."

And that, in a nutshell, explained why Maxine had allowed this unorthodox pen pal relationship to continue. Her heart broke for her son. Back when Hunter was in preschool, and even in kindergarten, all the kids seemed to be on equal ground. But it didn't take long for social awareness and parental attitudes to filter into the classroom. And, by third grade, Hunter suddenly didn't mesh very well with the other kids anymore.

At first Maxine had thought it was because of her. The other moms had always seemed to be a little threatened because she'd once been a college cheerleader and still looked the part. Plus, since she was single, she had the feeling that the other women went out of their way to make sure that she never spoke to their husbands alone—or even when under their direct supervision. So she and Hunter were rarely invited to any evening or family activities.

Then, when Maxine launched her cookie shop, she became so busy that she had very little time for playdates or other after-school events that kept all the other kids socially relevant.

She only wished she could keep Hunter as productive as the Sugar Falls Cookie Company. But her once-happy little boy had become increasingly introverted. And, as a result, he'd turned his attention more toward his computer and less toward the natural, outdoorsy life that their small-town community had to offer.

Luckily, she had her best girlfriends and her mother-in-law to help keep her son busy. And recently, she'd hired more employees to help out in the shop, which gave her a little more time for Hunter, although he didn't seem to want to do anything. But this pen pal business certainly had him perked up, so Maxine jumped on the chance to nurture his enthusiasm.

It was tough enough raising her son alone. Even if Bo hadn't wrapped his car around a tree in an overinflated exhibition of masculine pride, he probably wouldn't have stayed around long enough to help her raise Hunter anyway. But still, having to meet her son's pen pal face-to-face and playing chauffeur to some soldier they'd never met was one of those things no single-mom handbook had ever addressed.

So now she was winging it.

Back in September, she'd glanced at some of their earlier correspondence, if only to make sure this Cooper guy wasn't some predator or an otherwise bad influence on her sweet-but-naive son. The marine seemed on the up-and-up and she figured the relationship would run its course and fizzle out eventually. She wasn't happy about this unexpected shift in proximity or the significance Gunnery Sergeant Cooper was now having on both their lives.

Had she really let her son leave school early today for this?

"Did you print out that email with his itinerary?" she

asked, wishing she had given this whole airport to hospital run a little more consideration.

"Yeah, here it is." Hunter's growing fingers held it under her nose, and she remembered the way she used to kiss those little hands when he was a baby.

She almost missed the exit for the airport.

"Hunter, I'm driving. I can't read it right this second."

"Then why'd you ask me for it?"

"I wanted to know the exact flight details."

"He gets in at one forty-seven."

"Yeah, you told me that part already when you were practically shoving me out the door. But what airline is he coming in on, and are we supposed to take him straight to the hospital or what?"

"I don't know."

"What do you mean you don't know?" Maxine leaned her head against the leather headrest and slowly took three deep breaths. What she really wanted to ask was, *How do I keep forgetting that you're only ten and don't understand the ways of the world? And how do I let you talk me into these kinds of things?* But she saw the excitement on her son's face as he looked at the prized email again. "Just read me what it says."

To: hunterlovestherockies@hotmail.net
From: matthewcooper@usmc.mil
Re: Itinerary
Date: Jan 6
So my plane gets in on Thursday at 1:47pm. Don't worry about picking me up or anything. Boise Airport is both a civilian and a military airfield. It has military facilities on-site, so I can arrange for someone from the reserves unit there to take me to Shadowview.

I don't know what I plan to do after the surgeries are

over, but I doubt I'll get all the way up to Sugar Falls. We'll just see how my physical therapy goes. I'll look into getting a stateside cell phone when I arrive, so maybe hold off on calling the hospital for constant updates on my status.

Also, there's really no need to get me a Boise State T-shirt. Contrary to what you told me, I'm sure I'll manage to find appropriate Idaho clothes so that I won't "stick out like boobs on a bowling ball." You really need to stop repeating the dumb stuff you hear that Jake Marconi kid saying. You don't want to get your butt kicked by offending someone's girlfriend.

See you in a few days,

Cooper

"Hunter, that doesn't tell us anything. We should have checked his flight info. Do we even know if he's flying on a commercial airline? What if the plane is late? What if the hospital sent an ambulance to pick him up?"

"Then I'll ride to the hospital in the ambulance with him and you can pick me up there."

What world was her son living in that he thought she would ever approve of *that* harebrained idea?

But they had just pulled into the short-term parking area, so she was fully invested at this point and needed to keep her frustration in check.

"Here's the deal, Hunter. You can meet him. We'll say hi. But you're not spending any time alone with him."

"Mom, c'mon. Miss Gregson's brother is the military psychologist and personally screened all the marines before they were allowed to write to kids. They're fighting for our freedom. They're not weirdos or anything."

Her sweet son wouldn't know a weirdo if it jumped out of the Star Wars cantina scene and landed directly in his bed—right next to the wiener dog stuffed animal he still slept with every night.

She turned off the engine and shot him one last look, but he was already climbing into the backseat to retrieve the Welcome Home sign he'd worked on all last night. Then he was out the door and heading toward the arrivals terminal before she thought to ask him to show her a picture of what his pen pal looked like.

Cooper had barely hoisted the olive-green canvas duffel off the baggage claim conveyor belt and onto the floor beside him when he heard his name being shouted from behind the security guard checking luggage tags. All sound drowned out as a chubby ten-year-old waving a hand-painted poster board sign that said "Welcome Home, Cooper" ran at him.

If he hadn't set the wheel lock on the wheelchair when the airport personnel had parked him, he suspected the way Hunter launched his thick little body at him would've toppled them both over, chair and all. As it was, Cooper's injured leg screamed in protest at the sudden impact, but his heart leaped in joy at the way the kid's arms tightened around his neck.

He clung to the short boy dressed in a Colorado Rockies T-shirt, not sure why he was allowing himself to get so emotional in a random airport in the middle of America. Hunter was practically a stranger, yet at that second, he seemed closer to Cooper than anyone else in the world.

At every deployment homecoming he could remember, he'd stood to the side and watched the other marines reunite with their loved ones. He'd never begrudged his fellow soldiers their families or their loving receptions, but it had always made him feel a little… Well, it stirred up an ache somewhere deep inside to know that the only welcome he'd ever get—if he got one at all—was from a USO volunteer doling out a cup of coffee and a smile to anyone wearing a uniform looking the least bit lonely.

Something about squeezing Hunter back just as tightly as he was being embraced felt so right, and it made his eyes water a bit.

He needed to knock off all this sentimental crap. It must be the exhaustion and the jet lag. He ordered himself to man up and not become all weepy in public. Someone might think he was getting teary-eyed, and Cooper never cried. Not since... Well, not since he was practically too young to remember.

"I said you didn't have to come meet me." Cooper studied Hunter's freckled face and huge crooked-toothed grin. No one had ever been this excited to see him before.

"Are you kidding? I couldn't wait to meet you. I didn't even sleep last night. I made my mom get me out of class early so we'd be here on time."

At the mention of Hunter's mom, Cooper looked to his left and saw a tan pair of cowboy boots. His gaze traveled up the most toned and sexy legs he'd ever seen. Her jeans fit her like a second skin and rode low on her hips, the waist ending just below the hem of her white knitted sweater. Her white down-filled vest didn't cover up the fact that she had a knockout shape. Her beautiful face was surrounded by a mass of glorious blond curls. His fingers twitched at the thought of running through that silky hair, getting tangled in those...

Man, the image he'd conjured up of a dowdy overweight and overworked cookie baker didn't fit Maxine Walker one iota. In fact, she was stunning.

For a couple of elevated heartbeats, he hoped she would launch herself into his lap, just as her son had. But even if he'd been wrong about her appearance, Cooper had the woman's personality pegged right. She just stood to the side, distant and untouchable.

Her feminine hair and clothes gave off a warm impression, but the daintily sweater-clad arms crossed tightly around her midsection signaled she was anything but happy to be there.

Cooper had been in police work long enough to know when someone was trying to size him up for appraisal without actively making eye contact.

He ruffled Hunter's curly hair as he lifted the boy off his lap, then held out his hand to the woman who'd so obviously decided to close herself off to him. "I'm Matthew Cooper, ma'am."

Her palm was warm when it finally grasped his and he couldn't stop himself from thinking about how it had been snuggled against her slim waist just a second ago. "It's nice to meet you, Matt. I'm Maxine Walker."

He hated it when people called him Matt. Nobody but his mom and his childhood social worker had ever called him by his first name. And hearing the intimacy of his name from her lush pink lips would surely be his undoing. "Please, call me Cooper."

His leg was throbbing. He needed a shave and he had no doubt his eyes reflected his pain and his lack of sleep. Damn this stupid wheelchair and this stupid injury and everything else that suddenly made him feel like less of a man in her presence.

He hadn't been with a woman in a long time, but he needed to get things in perspective. A single mom with ties to the community—any community—wasn't for him. And the sooner he made that clear to himself, the better off he'd be.

Unfortunately, his voice came out a bit gruffer than he intended when he said, "You shouldn't have met me at the airport."

* * *

At that, Maxine stepped back and recrossed her arms, not sure what to do with her hands. "Well, it's a little too late for that, now, isn't it?" She'd driven all the way down the mountain to meet his flight and the man acted as if *they* were bothering *him*? What a tool.

A gorgeous, masculine tool with soft green eyes that made her heart bounce around like one of Hunter's water balloons trapped inside her rib cage.

Even with him seated in the wheelchair, she could see the man was tall and well-built. But just because he was attractive didn't mean she was any more at ease around him. In fact, that throbbing in her heart had her feeling all kinds of uncomfortable.

She'd already been on edge meeting this Gunny Cooper guy for the first time. And now, as he and Hunter were making a spectacle out of themselves in the middle of the baggage terminal, she didn't know where to look or where to stand.

One traveler had pulled out a cell phone, probably thinking he was recording some soldier's emotional homecoming, which meant there would be video footage of them on the internet within hours.

And what was with the "Call me Cooper" line? Could the guy be any more macho? Who went only by their last name? She understood military personnel and people who played team sports often went by their last names, but not in polite society.

Polite society? Geez, now she sounded like her former mother-in-law, Cessy. It was just that she wasn't Cooper's teammate or his squad leader.

Why was she already so damn frustrated, anyway? She wasn't annoyed with him for being in town or even for not communicating with her about the whole transportation plan. She wasn't even annoyed with him for having such broad shoulders or piercing eyes or hands that had made her own feel small and delicate.

Okay, so maybe that bugged her a little bit.

But hugging her son as if he were a loving father returned from the battle? Come on. Hunter was *her* child. She'd birthed him and raised him, and this testosterone-fueled stranger was acting as if he loved the boy more than she did.

"I just meant that I didn't want to be a bother or inconvenience anyone," he said as he reached up to ruffle Hunter's curly head again.

How could she detest someone who looked at her son with such affection? Why couldn't he have just said that in the first place instead of being so abrasive?

"Don't be crazy," Hunter said. "Of course I was going to be here to meet my best friend for the first time. I told my mom that I didn't care if she grounded me or if I had to ride my bike all the way down the mountain, but I was going to be here when your plane landed. No matter *what*."

"Sounds like your mom has her hands full with you, kiddo." The man helped Hunter as the boy struggled to lift the weight of the Marine Corps–issued duffel bag.

Did he just imply that Maxine couldn't handle her own child? Her eyes narrowed at the remark.

"Hunter, leave his bag alone. It's way too heavy for you." She didn't want Hunter dropping the guy's luggage and breaking something valuable. All she needed was a lawsuit.

"Oh, he's a tough kid, Mom. He can do it." Cooper smiled at Hunter. Wait. Had a grown man just called her *Mom*? Of all the patronizing insults! And was he purposely trying to override her authority with her own son? She'd hardly said anything at all to him. So why was the guy being so antagonistic?

Before Maxine could protest, Cooper began maneuvering his wheelchair himself as Hunter matched his wheeled pace toward the taxi stand, forcing her to trail behind, which probably suited Mr. Marine just fine. If he could've actually walked, he probably would've been leaping into a cab by now since he seemed so intent on getting away from her.

"Uh, hey guys," she called out as her boot heels clicked on the floor as she jogged to catch up with them. "Where are you going? What's the plan?"

Cooper used his hands to stop the wheels, then tried to execute some sort of turning maneuver, probably so he could face her. But he must not have been as experienced as he'd hoped because the brake handle caught midturn and it took him a few good thwacks to disengage it.

It served the show-off right.

"Well, I'm supposed to report to Shadowview by fifteen hundred hours so I can complete my admission paperwork. They said they'd send an ambulance to transport me, but I'm feeling fine so I think I'll just hail a cab."

The gray pallor of his skin was heightened by dark stubble along his jawline, and the man looked anything but robust. In fact, he looked as if he was in a world of pain. Of course, being the macho marine he clearly thought he was, he'd probably rather pass out or die before admitting it to her. She almost whipped out her phone to call for an ambulance right then and there, but her son's words interrupted her.

"You don't need to take a cab," Hunter told him. "My mom's car is super roomy. And since you can sit up just fine, you can ride with us. We'll take you to the hospital. Besides, it's on the way to Sugar Falls anyway."

No, no, no. Please say no, she willed him.

The man who called himself by his last name finally got his chair turned around just then and squinted those green eyes at her, as if trying to decipher the workings of her innermost thoughts. He must have read her mind because he lifted the corner of his mouth in a smirk that seemed to issue a challenge, and replied, "You know what, Hunter, that's a good point. I'd appreciate the lift."

Seriously? There was no way Cooper could possibly believe hitching a ride up the winding mountain road with her and her chatterbox son would be a wise decision. It was pretty obvious that he didn't like her, so why would he want to confine himself in a vehicle with her for the next thirty minutes? Unless, of course, he was accepting the invitation—which Hunter had no business offering—just to rattle her.

Maxine decided then and there that Cooper had to be the most contrary man she'd ever met. And the most attractive. But she'd never let him know that. And she'd be damned if she would let him think he was making her uncomfortable. Instead, she'd play the game his way. And she'd do it better.

Just in case he planned to stick around after his recovery—God forbid—then it was better to put him in his place now and let him know that she was calling the shots. It was petty and childish, for sure…but Gunny Heartthrob had started it.

She pulled the keys out of her purse and dangled them as she said, "Great, then it's all settled. I hope you don't mind women drivers."

Chapter Two

Maxine had barely driven away from the Shadowview Military Hospital when Hunter started in on all of his upcoming plans to visit his pen-pal-turned-best-friend. She nodded her head and made noncommittal "hmm" sounds every few minutes, but her teeth made deep indentations along her tongue as she kept herself from discrediting the man to his number one fan. She didn't want Hunter to get his hopes up, and prayed he would lose interest in his new hero by the time Cooper got his discharge papers.

When the boy's chattering finally slowed, she cranked up the radio volume, hoping the preprogrammed Motown station would get her back to her normally cheerful and positive self. But hearing The Miracles sing about really having a hold on her just hit too close to home. She reached out her hand to turn off the song, then froze, determined not to allow Cooper to have any type of hold on her.

Sweet mercy, even thinking the man's name made her

chest pound again. The guy was so beat up he could hardly write his signature on the admission forms, and Maxine experienced a twinge of regret for pushing him and that derelict airport-issued wheelchair to the limits when she'd quickened her steps and had forced his well-muscled arms to match her quick pace as they'd exited the baggage claim area. Really, though, it was his own fault for being so competitive—like every other male she knew—and refusing to let some female, even one who ran several miles a day, leave him in the dust.

Now, the closer she drove toward home, the more convinced she became that Cooper might not have been that much of a macho jerk if he'd been feeling better. So then why had she allowed him to get her so flustered? She tried to think of all the tidbits of information Hunter had told her about the marine these past few months. But her son usually talked nonstop, like he was doing now, and she figured it would just be easier to wait until Hunter went out with his grandmother tonight, and then go back and read the letters.

After all, it wasn't as if their correspondence was a secret. He'd shown the letters to her before—repeatedly. She just hadn't thought they'd been that important at the time and hadn't given them more than a passing glance. She pulled into her parking spot in the alley behind the Sugar Falls Cookie Company. Thank goodness her bakery closed every day at three o'clock. As soon as Hunter left for his regular Thursday night outing, she could slip right up to their renovated apartment upstairs and pour herself a glass of wine. Or a bottle.

"Your grandmother is going to be here to pick you up any minute. Take your backpack inside, then run up and change into that new sweater she bought you."

"Mom, that sweater is a joke," Hunter said as he got

out of the car and followed her inside the cool and quiet industrial-sized kitchen. "It's way too small and it has a picture of a bear throwing a football on the front. I can't wear that around town."

"Sweetie, sometimes we have to do things we don't want to do to make other people in our lives happy." *Like drive an hour to the airport to pick up an injured and cranky marine we've just met, then get insulted by his high-handed manliness as I drive him to the hospital— just to see my son smile.*

"Fiiine. Hey, I can't wait to tell Gram all about meeting Cooper. She said she'd drive me down to Shadowview to visit him after he has his surgery. And Aunt Kylie saw his picture and said he was a hottie. I bet she'd give me a ride to visit him, too. He's single, so maybe they could even go on a date or something when he gets all better."

A prickle of jealousy rose up along Maxine's spine. Her best friend Kylie was beautiful, and she did have an eye for the men. But the thought of her dating Cooper didn't sit well. Not that Maxine had any claim on the man. Heck, she wouldn't wish his grumpy bad attitude on anyone.

"I'll take you to see him, honey. You don't need to bother Gram or Aunt Kylie with that. Let's just wait and see how his surgeries go and what the doctors say before you make any plans to go visit. Besides, you have school and lots of other stuff you need to take care of first."

"Other stuff like what, Mom? I don't have any friends besides Jake. And it's not like you're going to let me play baseball this year, either."

"Hunter!" Maxine was tired of being made to look like the bad guy. "It's not like you're banned from sports or exercise. You could go running with me every afternoon. Or you could play tennis with Gram. And I bought you that Wii U sports game. I totally believe in exercising.

We've been over this. I just don't want you playing contact sports or getting a big ego the way most athletes do. There's so much more to life than sports."

"Not to your dad, there wasn't," a sugary voice sing-songed as the back door closed.

Maxine cringed as Cessy Walker, her former mother-in-law and Bo Walker's biggest fan, came strolling into the bakery to add her customary two cents.

"Your father loved football more than anything," Cessy added.

He definitely loved the game more than his wife and son, Maxine thought, with Bo's popularity coming in a close second. But she focused her attention on the woman who'd just entered the cookie shop.

Maxine nodded toward the stairway leading to their living quarters above the bakery. "Hunter, run upstairs to the apartment and change clothes. We can talk more about this when you come home tonight."

When she saw Cessy's gaze follow Hunter, she crossed her arms over her rib cage to hold her jittery emotions in check. No matter how helpful her mother-in-law was, the woman had a tendency to be every bit as overpowering as her perfume and opinions. Also, Maxine wasn't sure what Cessy already knew about the whole pen pal situation, but one thing she could count on was that Hunter's grandmother wouldn't like him having any heroes other than Bodrick "Bo" Walker, the legendary Sugar Falls High School quarterback and Boise State second-string tight end.

"Those Hudson Jeans look good on you," Cessy told Maxine. "I knew they would. I'll get you another pair when I go into the city next week."

"Thanks, but you don't need to do that. I don't need anything else. Really. You buy me and Hunter enough as it is." Maxine didn't have the heart to tell Cessy that with her cookie business booming the way it was, she probably now brought in more income than Cessy's monthly alimony checks and stock dividends combined.

"Honey, Bo wouldn't want his wife and only son running around in clothes off the discount store clearance racks."

In the zinger department, this was point one for Cessy. Maxine knew her mother-in-law wasn't trying to be insulting, but apparently the woman couldn't help sounding a little, well, snobbish.

"Besides," Cessy added, "I love doing this for you two. I'm the only family you have around."

Point two. Cessy always seemed to find ways to remind Maxine that she wasn't able to stay in frequent contact with her own scattered family.

When Hunter came back downstairs, pulling on the too-short waistband of the hated bear sweater, Maxine said, "Be good tonight for Gram."

Cessy ushered the boy out the back door and into her brand-new red Lexus. Her former mother-in-law got a new car every year, even though she was no longer married to the dealership's owner. Maxine suspected that a yearly lease was part of her last divorce settlement.

"And wear your seat belt," she added. "No TV or screen time tonight until you finish your homework."

Sometimes it seemed as though Maxine was constantly issuing orders, and it didn't sit well with her. She feared it was a residual from her days as a military brat. Maybe she shouldn't worry so much about Hunter. He was a good kid.

"Mom, I got it," Hunter said. "Stop stressing about me." Still, he lifted his head so she could drop a goodbye kiss on his cheek.

"Have him home before bedtime," Maxine called out,

but nobody in the Lexus seemed to hear her over the Barry Manilow CDs Cessy played constantly at high decibels.

As Maxine stood in the doorway, watching them drive away, a wave of loneliness swept over her. In the early mornings, when it was still dark outside, she loved the solitude as she creamed the butter and sugar in the warm industrial bakery kitchen, no sounds intruding to penetrate her thoughts. But she hated the empty feeling that engulfed her when that same silence enveloped her in the afternoons and evenings, when the outside sounds were a constant buzz of activity and a reminder that families everywhere were coming together to share the ups and downs of their days.

Normally, she would run upstairs to change into her workout clothes. She and her two best friends, Kylie and Mia, had a standing yoga date every Thursday evening. Afterward, they would have a dish session over dinner at their favorite local Italian place. She might not have the family home life she had always hoped for, but she'd sure done a fabulous job of creating a different sort of family—even if it was nontraditional.

However, now that she had met Cooper in person, her girlfriends would have to wait. Or she could call them and have them meet her here for an emergency strategy session.

She checked her watch. She had time to read just a few letters, so she went straight toward Hunter's room. On the bulletin board above his desk, she recognized the photo she hadn't given a second thought to when it'd arrived with the initial letter. In his camouflage uniform and helmet, he looked just like any other marine on duty.

But at some point in the past few months, that picture had been affixed right on top of an old copy of the *Sugar*

Falls Advocate article Cessy had given her grandson about high school tight end Bo Walker.

Cessy wouldn't like *that* placement too much.

A stack of APO addressed envelopes sat in a loose pile on top of the *Harry Potter* book that the school library had called about last week. Hunter had assured her he'd returned it on time, but maybe Maxine should've been checking his desk more often.

When she was one of seven siblings growing up in the cramped quarters of base housing, she'd promised herself that when she had kids of her own, they'd have privacy. She'd respect their boundaries.

But this was different. Wasn't it? She had a parental obligation to learn more about who her son wanted to spend time with. Besides, it wasn't as if Hunter kept to himself about these things. If it were up to him, he'd be shouting from the Victorian rooftops along Snowflake Boulevard about being the fifth grader with the coolest pen pal.

She looked at the postmarks until she found the one dated in September. That must be the first one. There was a picture still inside the envelope. She pulled out the photo and studied the desert camouflage of his uniform and the high and tight haircut of his dark hair. She'd seen enough military uniforms to last her a lifetime. Soldiers usually all looked the same to her. But the guy kneeling next to the dog seemed different. Maybe because she'd already seen that handsome face and strong jaw in person.

He wasn't smiling in the shot, but his arm was looped around the neck of a shaggy red dog, and his black Ray Bans were propped on his forehead. Something about the sadness in the marine's eyes called out to her, and she fingered the photo along the hardened chin as if she could force him to smile.

She scrolled through a few more and paused at one of the shots of him not wearing his customary sunglasses. She had to admit that he was good-looking in a tough, military sort of way.

Who was she kidding? The man was good-looking just off his long flight with beard stubble, jet lag and a bum leg. Of course he'd be even more handsome in uniform. She'd never been attracted to those types, though. They represented everything she'd tried to get away from during her childhood.

But somehow Cooper seemed different. He didn't really look as if he fit the military mold despite the regulation haircut. And mercy, Kylie was right—he really was hot. His running shorts showed off tan, well-muscled legs. She could see the outline of his washboard abs through his beige T-shirt.

It could just be the wine warming her up, but something pulsed in her lower lady parts. She hadn't experienced any pulsing down there in a long time, and she was uncomfortable with it. Maybe because it was a complete stranger who was making her feel this way. Or maybe because she was getting slightly turned on by his photos while sitting in her son's room surrounded by Angry Birds posters and Lego sets.

She needed to get ahold of herself. Or go out on a date once in a while.

Just then, a text message popped up on her smartphone. Kylie was running late and Mia's knee was too sore for yoga. Maxine took another sip of wine. She could either back out of their dinner plans now and sit in front of Hunter's computer screen staring at Gunny Heartthrob, or she could walk down the street and meet her friends at Patrelli's for pizza and another glass of wine.

Her nerves won out and she grabbed her heavy jacket

off the coatrack and practically ran out the door, trying to get as far away from her thoughts as she could.

To: hunterlovestherockies@hotmail.net
From: matthewcooper@usmc.mil
Re: Star Wars
Date: Jan 25
Hunter,
First of all, the femoral surgery went well. Dr. McCormick is supposed to be the top orthopedic surgeon in the Navy, and he expects me to recover quickly and undergo the knee replacement surgery just as well.

Second of all, Han Solo is in no way "more awesomer" than Luke Skywalker. You can't even compare the two. Han Solo is a smuggler. He isn't even a Jedi. Also, Luke is royalty, and he went through a lot of training. Han doesn't even have a light saber.

Third of all, I'm still learning to use Skype and I'm not used to it yet. And you have to promise that you'll get your mom's permission before we start talking on the computer like that.

Speaking of your mom, please thank her for sending that box of her cookies. When I shared them with all the guys on my floor, I was more popular than PFC Spooner, whose dad sends him magazines with— Well, I'll tell you about those when you're older.

I got the list you sent me with the names of every local police department that is hiring. I'm really not sure if I'm going to try to be a civvie cop. And I'm definitely not going to love Idaho "the way a drunk loves a martini." Does Jake Marconi even know what a martini is? Anyway, I'll keep you posted on when I can start having visitors.
Cooper

Cooper hadn't been lying to the kid. The surgery really had gone pretty well. It was too soon to tell if he'd make enough of a recovery to reenlist, but he didn't have the heart to tell Hunter that there was no way he planned to stay in Idaho permanently.

It was bad enough that he'd been putting off Hunter's visit, but, honestly, he didn't know if he could handle being around Maxine Walker again. The woman had brought out the worst in him that day at the baggage claim area, and it had been all he could take when she'd had to help lift him out of the airport-issued wheelchair and into her car.

She'd smelled as incredible as she looked. And the drive to the hospital had been just as intense as the woman's forced smile when Hunter had insisted on waiting for the admission paperwork to be completed and for the nurse to wheel him away to the orthopedic wing.

He didn't look forward to having to endure Maxine's stiff presence, but at the same time, he couldn't wait to see her again. To smell her again. Hell, to feel her hands on him again—even if it meant asking her to help him get out of this damn hospital bed to hit the head.

A light blinked on the bottom of his open laptop and he pulled the wheeled tray table closer to him.

He was receiving a Skype call from Dr. Gregson. The damn shrink was the one to blame for the whole mess. Back in September, Gregson had gone right over Cooper's head and his objections. He'd purposely sought out Cooper's commander to force him to participate in the pen pal program, knowing full well the honor-bound marine couldn't refuse a direct order.

As Cooper clicked on the mouse to connect their call, he had a lot more than some soul cleansing to discuss. There was hell to pay.

"Gregson," he bellowed, when the counselor's grainy image jumped onto his screen.

"How'd the surgery go, Gunny?"

Cooper relayed what Dr. McCormick had told him, including the part that his leg would never be 100 percent.

"I'm sorry to hear that. I know the Corps was your life."

"Yeah, well…" he cursed, though it hardly raised one of Dr. Gregson's eyebrows.

"Language, Gunny."

"Do you have to be such a sainted do-gooder all the time?"

"Do you have to be so cranky and miserable all the time? Here I thought you'd like Shadowview, being close to your pen pal and all that."

"That's another thing, Gregson. I'm still pissed about that whole program. I told you I didn't want to play pen pal to some kid. And yet you went up my chain of command and had me ordered to participate? You made me look like a loose cannon to Colonel Filden. And now he, and probably everybody else in my unit, thinks I'm some lonely PTSD candidate who needed a damn morale boost."

The only man Cooper had opened up to in his almost sixteen years in the Corps now sat behind a web cam with a self-righteous smirk on his saintly face. Gregson might make a good psychologist, but he was too softhearted to be a marine in a combat zone.

"I gave you the opportunity to accept graciously, Coop. You forced me to take it up with Colonel Filden."

It was hard to stay angry at Gregson when he simply sat there, passively and politely nodding his head and listening to Cooper's heated argument. Did they teach shrinks to smile and nod like that in grad school?

"Why are you still so upset about that?" Gregson asked. "What else did you have to do when you were off duty?

You never associated with any of your fellow troops. And you never went anywhere besides the chow hall and the weight room. And look at what you got out of the program."

"The decision should have been mine to make." Cooper tried to scratch under the bandage covering his recent incision. He knew Gregson was right and that meeting Hunter had been exactly what Cooper needed in his life at the time. Hell, his letters and emails with the boy were the only thing that got him through the aftermath of that explosion at the base, followed by a helo evac to Okinawa, where he'd had to stay while his body and leg stabilized enough to fly back to the States for surgery. If it hadn't been for Gregson, Cooper wouldn't have Hunter in his life.

Nor would his pain-addled mind be hosting those damn dreams of wrapping Maxine's sexy blond curls around his fingers. Being laid up in the hospital was making him stir-crazy and had his emotions spinning all over the place. Logically, he knew this situation that he'd landed in wasn't Gregson's fault, but the fact remained that his leg hurt, his pride hurt and he wanted to be mad at *someone*.

But Gregson didn't get riled. Instead, he changed the subject. "So when the knee replacement surgery is over, how long will it take to recover?"

"I'll stay in the hospital for a couple more weeks, doing rehab, and then they'll release me to go home, provided I come in for regular physical therapy sessions. But that could take weeks."

"Where would you stay?"

"I don't know. I guess a motel somewhere. Or I could probably rent a furnished apartment. I'm just trying to take everything one day at a time." Gregson knew enough about Cooper's background that he didn't have to expand on the fact that he didn't really have a home to go to. Even the apartment he'd once lived in as a boy never felt like a home since his mom had died and his stepdad never wanted him around. When Cooper had been married to Lindsay, she'd tried to make their tiny house on base a home, but it just always seemed so forced—as if they were just *playing* house. He was always more comfortable being on deployment than living with her, which was probably why their marriage didn't last.

"You know, my family lives in Boise. We have a cabin up in Sugar Falls you could use."

"I've got news for you, Gregson. Spending time in your quaint little vacation hideaway isn't going to give me back anything I've lost."

"Well, if you're going to keep your expectations low, you might as well do it in Sugar Falls, where it'll be more comfortable than some no-tell motel. Use the cabin, let your knee heal and think about your options if you can't reenlist. What are you so afraid of?"

Cooper bristled at the implication that he was afraid of anything. He had both a silver star and a purple heart to prove otherwise, and Gregson knew it. But Sugar Falls meant seeing Maxine on a regular basis and Cooper was smart enough to understand that hiding out in enemy territory wasn't brave, it was downright foolish.

"Forget the reverse psychology crap," he told the doctor. "I know they teach that BS in shrink school and Terrorist Interviewing 101, but it won't work on me."

"You and I both know the real reason you don't want to spend any time with the kid. You don't want to risk getting close to anyone. It might mean creating a crack in your hard shell of a heart."

Cooper gritted his teeth at the unwelcome analysis, his jaw fixed even harder than his alleged heart at that moment. Hell, he wasn't even a patient of Gregson's. The only thing they had in common was a proclivity for using the weight room after everyone else in their units had hit the rack.

When Cooper didn't respond, Gregson continued. "You know, maybe if you would've had a positive male role model back when *you* were a fatherless fifth grader, it wouldn't have stunted your emotional and social growth."

"Yeah, and maybe if you'd had a date or two while studying for your PhD, it wouldn't have stunted *your* ability to get laid." Cooper slammed the laptop closed.

"Uh, hello?" a feminine voice asked from behind the curtained partition that barely provided any privacy from the busy hospital floor.

"Yeah?" Cooper responded as he used the trapeze handle to lift himself up into a better position on the narrow bed.

Right before his brain registered the owner of the voice, Maxine Walker's very pretty face peeked around the curtain and her large blue eyes locked on to his. "Are we disturbing anything?"

He practically knocked the tray table over in his haste to pull the bed sheet over his exposed legs. Damn these short hospital gowns.

What was she doing here? And how much of his conversation had she just heard?

"Uh, no. I was just talking on Skype with my buddy and uh…" He trailed off as she lifted a perfectly arched eyebrow at the closed laptop. "What are you doing here?"

There he went again with that gruff accusatory tone, the defensive one he found himself reverting to whenever he was in an uncomfortable situation. He saw the ugly little cellophane-wrapped plant in her hands and tried to force his lips into a smile so he wouldn't seem like the world's biggest bastard for barking at her in such an ungrateful way.

"Hunter said you could have visitors, so I brought him down and…" She paused as her gaze swiveled around the room and then behind her into the corridor, as if she'd lost something. "Well, he was with me just a second ago. Maybe I should go find him."

She turned to walk out, and he pulled himself up as if he could will his useless body to physically stop her from leaving. "Wait, you don't have to go. I mean, I'm sure he just got distracted and will be along any minute." Cooper nodded his head toward the wilted green thing in the plastic pot. "Is that for me?"

"Oh, this? It's just a little something to cheer up your room." She walked toward the small window and set the plant on a bare cabinet, causing some curling leaves to fall off their stems.

He'd seen interrogation huts in third world countries more cheerful than that dying shrub. But he thanked her all the same.

"So, the surgery went okay?" Now that her hands were empty, she'd reverted back to that same stance she'd displayed at the airport—arms crossed tightly across her torso.

"I guess so. One down and one to go. I guess the real recovery will start after that."

"Hey," Hunter interrupted, as he finally breezed in past the curtain. "There's a guy down the hall with the coolest robot legs, and they have him doing jumping jacks and leg squats and all kinds of things. He showed me how the new joints are like titanium-powered springs, and now he's like an incredible bionic man. Maybe they'll give you some legs like that, Coop."

As exciting as the kid made it sound, Cooper needed the reminder that he was lucky to still have all of his own limbs. A lot of soldiers had injuries so much worse than his. "I don't know, little man. I'm kinda attached to these legs right here." Cooper patted the sheet that he'd finally gotten into place.

"Can I see your stitches?"

"Hunter." Maxine blushed, and Cooper enjoyed seeing the pink flush stain her cheeks. It made her seem warmer somehow. "Leave his bandage alone. He probably needs his rest."

"I'm okay," he said, wanting to reassure Maxine that her son didn't bother him in the least. He pulled the sheet back so Hunter could get his curiosity fix.

"Oh, wow, they had to shave your leg and everything. Just like a girl." Hunter screwed up his chubby little face in disgust. "Dr. McCormick didn't tell me about *that* part."

"When did you talk to my surgeon?" Cooper asked. Maxine's puzzled expression must have matched his own.

"When I called him yesterday to ask how your surgery went and to see when we could come visit. He said today was fine, so Mom brought me down."

Maxine raised her shoulders and shook her head, as if to tell him she had no idea her ten-year-old son was capable of navigating his way through a busy hospital's switchboards and acquiring confidential patient information. But Cooper wasn't the least bit surprised. In fact, he wouldn't put it past Hunter to know what he'd had for breakfast, how many times the nurses had changed his IV bag and when his next sponge bath was scheduled.

Looking at Maxine, whose arms were now akimbo in confusion, and whose perfectly formed breasts were on proud display under her snug white cotton top, he couldn't help but wish that she could be the one to assist him at bath time.

"I brought you my *Lord of the Rings* DVD series." Hunter's voice brought Cooper back to reality. "My mom got you that plant. It looked better when she picked it out in the grocery store, but Gram says Mom has a black thumb and kills everything she touches."

"Well, it's the thought that counts," Cooper said, trying to muster up something positive to say. He couldn't very well agree with Hunter's grandmother, could he?

"Now you sound like Mom when she makes me wear the stupid clothes Gram picks out."

The little white phone by his bedside rang just then, and before Coop could move, Hunter jumped to answer it. "Gunnery Sergeant Matthew Cooper's room."

"Sorry," Maxine whispered as her son spoke into the corded receiver. "I thought you were the one who told him he could visit. I didn't know he was calling your doctor directly."

"It's okay," Cooper whispered back, actually surprised by how much seeing them both had boosted his spirits.

"Yeah, he's right here." Hunter spoke with the importance of an adjutant screening a four-star general's call. "But he still has the same ole boring human legs. Okay, hold on, Colonel Filden."

Cooper grabbed the phone from Hunter's hand and covered the mouthpiece as he spoke to his guests. "Thanks for coming to visit, but I have to take this call."

"Okay, I'll come back in a couple of days," Hunter promised, but Maxine shook her head at the boy while attempting to quietly lead him out of the room.

He hoped they understood that he wasn't trying to dismiss them out of rudeness. But this was possibly the call that would decide his entire future. And no matter how cool Hunter was—or how pretty his mom—Coop wanted nothing more than to get the hell out of here, stat.

Chapter Three

"Hello, sir," Cooper finally said into the receiver once he knew Maxine and Hunter were well on their way down the hall.

The men exchanged general pleasantries for all of twenty seconds before his commanding officer finally cut to the chase.

"Here's the bottom line," Filden said. "They're not needing as many soldiers, and they're getting real stingy with the retirement pay. Your record speaks for itself. You're a phenomenal marine. An asset to the squadron. Your men respect you and look up to you. I did my best to push for your reenlistment, but it doesn't look good. Hell, if it were up to me, you would've been promoted to First Sergeant after your last deployment. But when you add this new injury to the mix, there's just no way the government is willing to take the gamble. Anyway, nothing's official yet, but I figured I'd give you a heads-up so you could start thinking about your future and any possibilities that may arise."

The itch near Cooper's incision flared up, and he wanted to throw the phone across the room and rip his bandage off. But he took the conversation like a man. As much as Cooper hated hearing the truth, he was grateful the colonel wasn't shining him on. "I appreciate your candor, sir."

"You're made for police work, Gunny. And right now, just about every major department and agency stateside is hiring cops. I'm just saying it's not a bad idea to put some feelers out. See if there's anything open in your hometown."

"Yes, sir," Cooper said, knowing full well he'd never step foot in his old neighborhood if he could help it. The truth of the matter was that Cooper didn't have a home, let alone a hometown. Nor did he have anyone he could talk to about what his options were.

"I'll let you know if I hear anything different," Filden added. "But a marine is always ready for anything, right?"

"Right, sir. Semper Fi."

Cooper was almost surprised at the gentle way he eased the receiver down. Probably because he'd never wanted to throw anything so badly in his life.

So there it was. One minute he'd been out for a jog along the base perimeter with his dog, Helix. The next minute, a sixteen-year career in the Corps was gone in the flash of a detonated suicide bomb strapped to some poor insurgent's chest.

To: matthewcooper@usmc.mil
From: hunterlovestherockies@hotmail.net
Re: Surgery
Date: March 1

I didn't know that Miss Gregson's family has a cabin up here in Sugar Falls. That's so cool that they're letting you stay in it when you get out of the hospital. I still think you should stay with me and my mom so we can take care of you and make sure you don't fall or bust your knee back open. But at least we'll be close enough to see each other every day.

How long are you going to be able to stay? I know you're bummed about being discharged from the marines, but there are some real great cop jobs all over Idaho. Did you check out any of those applications I printed out for you?

Anyway, me and my mom will pick you up on Sunday and give you a ride to the cabin. Or to our house if you get smart and change your mind. And don't forget, you're gonna play catch with me when your leg is better. See ya,
Hunter

No! No, no, no.
What had Hunter done?

He'd left his computer on when he'd gone to Boise with Cessy to see the latest superhero movie, and Maxine had only come in to collect the smelly socks and inside-out pants that were piling up in the corner.

But his laptop screen was open to his outbox and she soon realized the perfect small town world she'd created for herself and her son was about to change.

She went to the kitchen and grabbed a bag of barbecue potato chips before coming back to Hunter's room to re-read the email her son had sent that afternoon.

For years, people had been telling her that Hunter needed a positive male role model in his life. She knew some manly influence wasn't necessarily a cause for alarm, but she wanted to be the one to decide who exerted that influence.

And now Hunter had invited this jerk to their hometown to recover from his surgery. He'd even volunteered *her* to pick the guy up at the hospital! She should have grounded him after that airport ride stunt, because apparently the boy hadn't learned his lesson.

Geez, what should she do? She wanted to call someone to ask for advice, but who?

Her friend Mia understood kids. But Mia had a late-night dance class. Kylie was probably on a date, and Cessy's advice was never an option, even if her mother-in-law wasn't with Hunter. It sucked that her son certainly didn't have a father she could share her parenting concerns with.

That was probably the reason Hunter had gotten into this situation in the first place. No father figure. And no matter how hard Maxine had tried to be both mom and dad, she must not have pulled it off. There was obviously something lacking in Hunter's life that drew him to some random soldier like a heat-seeking missile.

After the day that Cooper had shooed them out of his room to take a phone call, she vowed she wouldn't put herself in the same room as the marine again. And she hadn't. Each time she'd taken Hunter to visit, which had been every week for over a month, she would walk the boy to Cooper's room and then wait for her son out in the small lobby near the nurses' station.

Just then, a window flashed in the bottom of the screen, signaling an incoming Skype call from Cooper.

She wanted to close the lid, but she couldn't avoid the guy any longer. It would be better to get this matter settled before Gunny Heartthrob muscled his way into her their everyday lives. Her fingers paused over the mouse before she slowly moved it to the box and clicked.

The chat screen shot to life and Maxine was immediately faced with a live version of her son's pen pal soldier.

"Hey, kid." The grainy image displayed the same lonely eyes she'd seen in that one picture, but his head was lying back against a white sheet on a hospital bed. That is, until he braced himself up on his elbow, narrowed his eyes and gazed into the screen. "Oh. Hi."

"Hi. Hunter's out. I was just in his room, uh, cleaning." Geez, she sounded as lame as she looked. In the small box in the corner, Maxine recognized herself, with her curly blond hair pulled messily into a ponytail on top of her head.

Was that how she really looked on a webcam? She should've put on some lip gloss instead of going for the chips. Speaking of which, she slowly slid the now-empty bag out of view from the camera.

Of course, Cooper looked great. He was 100 percent male and even in a hospital bed, he was still as gorgeous as hell. She didn't need him running around her town all healthy and virile.

Ugh. She needed to get a grip. And not just of the rustling bag that was teetering precariously off the edge of the desk.

"So, I hear you're getting discharged soon," she said, when it appeared that Cooper wasn't going to start the conversation.

"Yep. I was trying to stay in until I could retire, but I guess…stuff happens." He appeared to lose his balance and cursed, then looked a little embarrassed. "Look, I don't usually cuss like that in front of your son. Seeing you on my screen just kind of caught me…ah…off guard."

This was her opportunity to tell him that this whole

Sugar Falls visit had caught *her* off guard and wasn't such a great idea. But at that exact moment, Hunter walked into the room.

She hadn't even heard him enter the apartment because she'd been staring so intently at Coop's beard stubble and wondering what it would feel like rubbing against her...

Whoa. She was *not* going there. Especially now that her son was present.

"Oh, cool, you're talking to Cooper. Hey, Coop, are you coming to Sugar Falls?"

Maxine hadn't even had the chance to cast her son a reprimanding look before Hunter leaned over, and then practically crawled over her to get in view of the tiny webcamera.

"What's up, little man?" It was hard to register on the megapixels blurring on the screen, but she was sure that the look in Cooper's eye softened when he saw Hunter. His tone of voice certainly did. "I was just going to talk to your mom about that."

But before Maxine could get any answers, Cessy popped her perfectly coiffed head in the door, and Maxine jumped up to hustle her former mother-in-law out of the room.

She wasn't sure why she didn't want the woman to interact with their pen pal—

Wait! When did Cooper become *theirs*?

Whatever. All she knew was that the less Cessy was involved, the better.

Besides, it wasn't as if Maxine had anything to hide. She wasn't cheating on Bo or anything. Bo was dead. And Cooper wasn't even in the running as a candidate to replace her husband. As if she would ever get married again. That ship had sailed.

Maxine steered Hunter's grandmother toward the back

door as Cessy talked incessantly about her latest shopping spree. Hopefully, the older lady didn't even realize that her grandson just ditched her to do some online hero-worshipping. Or that her former daughter-in-law was blushing like a schoolgirl with her first crush.

She needed to get Cessy out the door so she could go back and tell that marine that under no circumstances was he to come visit. So she hugged the woman goodbye and thanked her repeatedly for taking Hunter shopping—yet again. But before she could turn the lock, Maxine's cell phone vibrated.

Kylie.

Maybe Maxine should ask her friend for a quick opinion before rejoining the Skype chat. She had to talk to someone, even if it was her chronically single best friend.

"Is the date over?" Maxine asked instead of answering with a polite hello.

"No, I just snuck away and am debating whether or not my big ole booty will get stuck if I try to crawl through this bathroom window."

Maxine reached into the back of her pantry and found a forgotten snack-sized package of pretzels. The empty bag of chips she'd left by Hunter's computer had been the last of her emergency stash.

"Why do I do this to myself?" Kylie asked. "Frankie is a tax attorney I met at that seminar last week. Who knew a guy with such a party name could deliver a mind-numbing monologue on the importance of the Foreign Account Tax Compliance Act through a mouth stuffed with sautéed spinach in chimichurri sauce? I'm about to—"

"Listen," Maxine interrupted. Kylie's *Bad Date Story From Hell: Volume 89* would just have to wait until tomorrow. "I need your advice. Hunter is trying to talk Cooper into coming to Sugar Falls after he gets discharged from the hospital."

"You mean Gunny Heartthrob?"

Maxine nearly dropped her phone. "Stop calling him that."

"You called him that first. You told us he literally made your heart throb when you met him. Anyway, if he comes to town, would he be staying at your place? I have a sexy nurse's costume you could borrow to help him on his road to recovery."

"Kylie! Are you serious? I have a son. Even if I wanted to, which I don't, I can't be shacking up with some marine from who knows where."

"Listen, Max, the guy seems cool. Hunter thinks the world of him, and I hate to point out the obvious, but that poor boy needs a man to talk to. Better a military cop than some lowlife gangbanging druggie."

Great. Maxine didn't need the reminder that he was in the military *and* a cop. Matthew Cooper probably couldn't cram any more testosterone into his camouflage pants if he tried.

"Where would he find a lowlife gangbanging druggie in Sugar Falls?" she asked her friend, before realizing they were getting completely sidetracked.

"That's a good point. This town can be so boring sometimes."

"Kylie, focus. Hunter invited this man to come here."

"So what? Hunter also asked Jorge de la Rosa from the Colorado Rockies to come to his class presentation for that baseball book report he did. De la Rosa didn't show and this guy probably won't, either."

"You may be wrong."

"Do you think he's actually coming?" Kylie suddenly

seemed way too perky. Maxine tamped down the jealousy that crept its way around her closed-off heart.

"I don't know. I don't think so. That's what I need to ask you about." She quickly filled her friend in, explaining about Hunter's email and then the awkward Skype session.

"I bet Hunter would be thrilled to see his pen pal more often."

"Well, *he'd* be the only one."

"Max, just because the guy rubs you the wrong way doesn't mean he's bad for your son."

She knew what Kylie said was true, but it was still a tough pill to swallow. "So you don't think I should go back in there and explain that it's a bad idea for him to come out to visit?"

"Is it?"

"Is it what?"

Kylie sighed, almost as if she'd rather get back to Frankie and foreign tax compliance than have this conversation that was clearly a life-altering event in Maxine's opinion.

"Is it such a bad thing if this guy comes to Sugar Falls for a couple of weeks? Hunter obviously adores him, and the guy seems pretty stand-up. Why not let them hang out? It's not like you can kill off their friendship at this point. Hunter would be devastated."

Her friend was right. "I don't want to hurt my son, but how can I protect him? What if Coop doesn't live up to the hype? As far as I'm concerned, Hunter has already been let down by one man in his life. He doesn't need any more disappointment."

"Look, maybe this guy has absolutely no intention of coming out to visit. Just go back in and talk to him. Get to know the man a little bit better so you can become comfortable with the relationship—whatever that may be. Then let it fizzle out on its own." She sighed dramatically. "Gotta go. Chimichurri teeth are coming this way. Let me know what happens."

The call disconnected. Maybe Kylie was right. Her friend sucked at her own relationships, but was pretty good at understanding other people and human nature.

Maxine finished the rest of the pretzels and walked slowly down the hall toward her son's room, her bare feet padding along the hardwood floor the only sound she heard. There wasn't any more talking going on and she wondered if the chat was over already.

She peeked in and saw her sweet little ten-year-old lying on his bed, reading the new Wimpy Kid book Cessy must have bought for him on their shopping trip—probably as a bribe to get him to wear the red-and-orange sneakers she thought were the latest and coolest fashion.

That was just as well. She leaned against the doorjamb. Maxine'd had too much for one night. Too much worry, too much sexy marine.

She should just sleep on it and let all the conflicting thoughts racing in her brain simmer down before she talked to Hunter. She worked best on her problems early in the morning when she was alone in her bakery, anyway.

She just hoped Cooper hadn't already let Hunter talk him into coming to Sugar Falls. After all, what could their cozy Idaho town possibly offer a man like him?

What indeed.

Yet, two days later, on Sunday afternoon, Maxine watched as Cooper slowly limped along next to her son, holding his discharge papers and the ugly little plant that was starting to perk back to life. Hunter was once again trying to carry the man's duffel bag, and she shoved her hands into the pockets of her short, blousy white dress to keep from reaching out to help her son.

"So I figured you could just ride back up the mountain with us," Hunter told his pen pal. "You won't need a rental car or nothing because you can just borrow my mom's car if you need to go somewhere."

"Honey, let Cooper plan his own stay in Sugar Falls," she said as they climbed into her SUV. It *was* just a stay, she hoped. A very, very short stay. "If he wants to get a rental car, he should do that. Besides, I need my car, and we don't want him getting stuck without transportation."

She definitely didn't want him stuck in *her* town with *her* son and *her* friends and *her* neighbors. None of them needed this guy staying too long. He could just keep going along his merry little macho way.

In fact, she'd had no intention of even coming to the hospital to pick him up. But when she'd found out Hunter had asked both Cessy and Kylie to give him a ride, she wasn't about to allow her mother-in-law to encourage the male bonding. And as much as she loved her man-crazy best friend, she wasn't going to let Kylie flirt with the guy they'd gotten in the embarrassing habit of calling Gunny Heartthrob.

And like it or not, those eyes of his certainly had a way of making her heart thump all around her rib cage.

"I'm staying at Drew Gregson's cabin, up off Sweetwater Bend and Snowflake Boulevard. He said there's an old Jeep up there I could use while I'm in town, so don't worry about me." When he smiled at Hunter, Maxine's heart thawed for a second. But only a second.

Jeep or no, she didn't want the man getting too comfortable in Sugar Falls.

The drive up the mountain was pure torture for Cooper. And not because of Maxine's infuriatingly slow driving, which he decided she must be doing on purpose.

The woman smelled like vanilla and every cozy kitchen aroma he'd ever wished to come home to when he'd been a child, fending for himself. But that was where any sense of hearth and home ended.

Why was she being so cold toward him? Not that he wanted her to flirt or try and get too close, but what would it hurt for her to make some sort of small talk? Or at the very least, loosen her white-knuckle grip on the steering wheel?

It was bad enough that she'd refused to enter his hospital room whenever she'd brought Hunter to visit. Was being in his presence that horrible of an inconvenience for her?

In fact, he'd wanted to decline the offer of a ride up to the cabin, but a little piece of him wanted to be near her, even if it meant enduring her standoffish attitude.

Luckily, Hunter had talked nonstop the entire twenty-five minutes it took to get up the mountain, which helped to alleviate the tension between the two adults in the front seat.

As they approached civilization, she finally picked up speed. He noted a large timber-and-stone sign welcoming travelers to Sugar Falls, home of skiing, kayaking and the Sugar Falls Cookie Company.

Whoa, the cookie queen must be a pretty big deal in town if her company got an honorary mention on the welcome billboard.

Once inside the city limits, Hunter's chatter took on a faster pace. "There's my school and the fire department and the post office. And this is what we consider downtown. See the yellow building over there? That's my mom's cookie shop. We live in the upstairs part. My room is the second window on top."

Cooper merely nodded as Maxine accelerated her SUV

through what he suspected was a twenty-five mile-per-hour area. She sure seemed to be in a hurry to get him through what had to be familiar surroundings and, most likely, her comfort zone. He didn't think it was possible, but her hands gripped even tighter on the wheel as she ran through a yellow light at the main intersection.

"There's Patrelli's," Hunter continued. "It's my favorite pizza place. And that's Noodie's Ice Cream Shoppe, but I don't know why they spell it with an extra *P* and *E*. We get our groceries here at Duncan's Market... Hey, Mom, that was Mr. Jonesy you almost cut off. Slow down, Cooper can't see everything if you're driving so fast."

The cookie queen took three deep breaths, and then eased her cowboy boot off the accelerator. Her tanned and toned legs were bare and the hem of her dress was riding high on her thigh. But Cooper had a feeling that sexy length of skin was all she would ever reveal of herself.

Cooper didn't say a word. The woman obviously wanted to get rid of him. Well, he'd be just as obliged to get out of this four-wheeled, leather-interior death trap.

Hunter, as if finally cuing in on his mom's tension and Cooper's discomfort, fell silent, allowing the marine to take in the lay of the land.

He thought of Gregson, who'd coerced him to recuperate in Buttsville, Idaho, instead of a tropical resort in Tahiti. When he was still in the hospital, Cooper had talked on Skype with the psychologist, who'd filled him in with stories about growing up in Boise and their cabin up in the mountains of Sugar Falls.

Gregson had reminisced about the town being home to some of the best memories of his childhood. There was fishing and hiking and Norman Rockwell nonsense galore. *Must've been nice to have a childhood like that.*

Sugar Falls wasn't as remote as he'd expected and it

definitely had a lot more character than any place he was used to. No two Victorian-style buildings were alike, providing a fresh boon of color and shops and restaurants in the middle of the rugged green wilderness. Gregson said hipsters flocked here for weekend vacations, and Cooper could see why. In fact, the shrink said he planned to move to the cabin himself when his tour was up in July. He had even put in a transfer request to be stationed at Shadowview.

But no matter how much the quiet town might appeal to the homeless, former marine, Cooper intended to be long gone from here before then.

He reminded himself that the only reason he was staying in Sugar Falls was because *he* wanted to. Not because some little boy wanted to hang out with him—and not because he liked hearing some homesick buddy's stories about an idyllic vacation town. And it for sure wasn't because he wanted to spend more time with the sexy cookie queen.

They reached the other side of town, which probably took all of forty-five seconds and three seemingly unnecessary stoplights, and Hunter tapped him on the shoulder. When Cooper turned to look in the backseat, the boy silently pointed out a Little League field that was coming back to life after a snowy winter. Apparently, the normally yappy kid didn't want his mom to know that they were even looking at something sports related.

That would be the first thing Cooper changed while he was in town. Not that he had any business getting involved in Hunter and Maxine's relationship. It wasn't as if he was one of those interfering social workers he'd hated back in the day. But playing a little catch with the kid wouldn't be overstepping his bounds, right?

Maybe that sporting goods shop he'd spotted on Snowflake Boulevard sold baseball gloves, and not just the snowboards and kayaks that lined the outside walls. He made a mental note to check that place out. He'd been in town less than three minutes and already he was planning his first covert op.

They continued another two miles up the mountain before Maxine swung a sharp right turn onto a small dirt street that looked more like a wilderness trail. There was no signage, so Cooper probably would've passed the road leading to the cabin if he'd been driving himself.

They bumped over several deep gouges and potholes, his injured knee absorbing every impact. Damn. Was she purposely aiming at all those bumps? If he hadn't seen her raise her sunglasses and lean forward over the steering wheel to carefully navigate the narrow lane that was practically enclosed with pine and larch trees, he would have thought so.

"Wow, this place is awesome!" Hunter jumped out of the car before his mom put it in Park.

Cooper had seen a stream running along the main road, but now that he opened the car door, he could tell by the sound of running water that it had to be close to the house.

The log cabin was somewhat plain and shaped like a box, but it had big paned windows and a covered patio. From the outside it appeared pretty simple and well maintained, which, coupled with the tranquil melody of the nearby stream, allowed him to let out his pent-up breath and relax his shoulders.

"Hunter," Maxine said, "get back in the car. We can't stay. We're supposed to be having Sunday dinner at Gram's house."

"Hey, Coop, you want to come over to my Gram's house for dinner tonight?"

Before Cooper could answer, Maxine placed an arm

around her son and spoke quietly but apparently firmly, causing the boy to nod his head and scuff his sneaker toe at a stone embedded in the driveway.

He assumed his little buddy was getting a talking-to about inviting people over without asking permission. He didn't want to be the cause of any more problems between the boy and his mother, so Cooper stretched and purposely yawned. "Actually, my knee is killing me and I really need to get some sleep. Maybe you can come see the place later this week. We can do some exploring and maybe catch a few fish. I'll talk to your mom, and we'll figure out a time that works for both of us."

"Okay." The boy lowered his head in dejection and gave Cooper a hug before climbing in the front seat. "I'll see you later."

Cooper thought Maxine would've appreciated his help in defusing the situation and giving her an excuse to get the hell away from him, but instead of appearing relieved, her brows drew tightly together over confused eyes.

When he brushed past her on his way to the rear of the vehicle, she jumped out of his way. "Where are you going?"

"To get my duffel out of the back of your car, if that's okay with you."

"Oh. Yeah. Of course. You just startled me."

The woman was a jumble of nerves. She'd been like an ice queen throughout the drive and was now pacing around him like a popcorn kernel about to pop.

He grabbed his bag and barely had it out of the back when she reached for the handle on the rear hatch and nearly slammed it down on him.

He lowered his voice so Hunter wouldn't hear him. "I get it, lady. You don't want me around. But can you at least let me get my gear out of your car before you back over me and leave my body up here in the Idaho mountains?"

"I would never back over you."

"Could have fooled me," he muttered.

She whipped around and pierced him with those cold blue eyes. "I wouldn't want any of those perfect muscles to dent my fenders." Then she climbed back in the car and was backing out onto the graveled drive much quicker than she'd navigated it while driving forward.

Well, at least she'd noticed his muscles. And she'd thought they were strong enough to dent her car. He'd take that as a compliment.

Smiling, he carried his bag onto the porch and found the green door unlocked. This town might be like Mayberry RFD, but he was no Barney Fife. He kept his dead bolts in place and his gun nearby no matter where he was.

He flicked a switch inside the doorway, illuminating the cabin, where several rag rugs adorned the hardwood floor and a denim-covered sofa sat in front of a stone fireplace. The kitchen and dining room were open and part of the living area, which had beige-colored walls and dark beamed ceilings.

The rustic cabin was deceptively appealing. Just like the woman who'd driven him here. Even though Maxine Walker seemed like a contemporary replica of one of those 1950's sitcom mother figures baking cookies and doting on her kid, she was beautiful and cold just like the inside of this house, in which he'd be staying for who knew how long.

Damn. He needed to stop thinking of her and why he was even in Sugar Falls, and get a fire started before he froze. It might be sunny outside during the spring day, but obviously the closed up cabin retained the chill of the night air. He must've gotten soft sitting in that military hospital because he was losing his edge on surviving in the elements.

A small stack of chopped wood, as well as kindling and a book of matches, rested next to the fireplace. So he knelt by the open hearth and proceeded to make a fire. When the flame caught hold, he stood back and put his hands out to absorb some of the heat.

Not bad for someone who'd grown up a city boy. Actually, if he was honest, he hadn't really grown up until he'd joined the Corps. Being a marine taught him everything he ever needed to know about surviving in the world.

So then, how would he survive now that he was no longer a marine?

He looked around the comfortable cabin. Gregson had underrepresented how nice the place was. Heck, the psychologist had underrepresented how nice the whole area was. Not nice as in fancy, but nice as in, well, cozy.

He cursed softly to himself, not wanting to think of the town or the cabin as anything other than practical.

Once Cooper assured himself that the fire would continue to blaze without fizzling out, he walked over to the kitchen, opened the pantry and took stock of what groceries he'd need from the small market in town. There was a bottle of Scotch, which could come in handy. Other than that, there were some canned goods—mostly tuna and green beans—and a jar of peanut butter. He'd made do with a lot worse.

The sun had already set and he wasn't sure what time this charming but rinky-dink town closed up for the night. But the lack of sleep on the flight, plus the mountain air and oxygen level was already doing a number on him. The grocery shopping would have to wait until morning.

The refrigerator was clean, but totally empty and unplugged. He shoved the cord into the wall and it hummed to life.

He rummaged in the drawers for a can opener and fork and was surprised at how organized and well-equipped the tiny kitchen was. According to Gregson, the cabin hadn't been used in years. The doctor's sister—Hunter's teacher—checked on it regularly, but she lived in Boise and commuted to work.

As much as Cooper wanted to ruffle Maxine's feathers and accept Hunter's invitation for a home-cooked dinner, he hadn't lied about his excuse—he really did want to get some sleep. He was practically operating on fumes and his knee was throbbing.

While standing at the kitchen counter, he ate the tuna straight from the can. Then he took two of his pain meds and guzzled down a glass of ice-cold tap water. Damn, that was good—probably because it was so pure and came straight from its source, the Sugar Falls River.

The fire was doing its job and the cabin was much warmer now. He just hoped the pills worked as well. Maybe a liquid chaser would do the trick. He'd like nothing better than to crash until morning.

After pouring himself three fingers of Scotch—for medicinal purposes only—he carried his drink and his duffel to the small hallway and looked at his bedroom options. The one on the left contained a set of quilt-covered bunk beds, but the one on the right, with a huge king-size bed made out of split logs and covered with a fluffy goose down comforter, won out.

He tossed all of his worldly possessions—which fit nicely into the green canvas bag—onto a chair in the corner before downing the Scotch, stripping off his clothes and slipping between the sheets. It must've been the exhaustion coupled with the medication and the booze that made him long for a sexy, curly haired blonde to slide in next to him and, for once, flash him a smile.

Chapter Four

"Mom, why did you have to be so mean to Cooper? Now he'll probably hate us and want to leave town first thing tomorrow morning."

Hunter was right, and Maxine had no good explanation to give for her ill-mannered behavior. Well, no explanation that a ten-year-old boy without a clue about human attraction could understand.

She herself didn't even understand it. There was something about Cooper that set her on edge. No man had ever frustrated her so much, and she'd been married to the King of Frustration.

Maybe it was because she was so damn attracted to Cooper. Bo had been good-looking in a fresh young college student sort of way. But Cooper was a *man*. Not to mention he related to her son in a way nobody else ever had. How could that not influence Maxine's heart just a little?

"I'm sorry, Hunter. Cooper is your friend, and I didn't want to get in the way, so I kept quiet so you two could talk. Besides, I don't really know him as well as you, and I guess I was nervous. Plus, I didn't want to be late to Gram's house for dinner."

There. That was a mostly honest answer.

"But, Mom, we just left him at the cabin without even making sure he got inside okay. What if the power is out or if he doesn't have any groceries or anything to eat in there?"

Bless her son for being so thoughtful. But maybe Gunny Heartthrob should have thought about that before he purposely accepted a ride she'd never offered—twice.

"There's a Jeep he planned to use, remember? And you gave him directions back to town so he could find his way around and buy himself whatever he needed. I'm sure he'll be fine, kiddo."

"But what if his knee hurts too much to drive or the Jeep doesn't run? Or what if it was stolen by robbers? Wait, what if a band of robbers had been using that cabin for their hideout, and we just left Cooper there all alone with no phone and no way out? Or worse! What if the robbers are really zombies who steal people's hearts for the zombie science experiments they're conducting? Mom, we have to go back and get him."

"Hunter, I'm sure there aren't any robbers or zombies in the cabin." Besides, the zombies would be in for a big disappointment when they realized that Cooper didn't seem to have much of a heart, but Maxine kept that opinion to herself. "Even if there were problems with the electricity or the Jeep, Cooper was a marine. I'm sure he can handle himself out there in the woods."

"But what if…"

"Enough, Hunter." Maxine stopped her son's tirade

when she saw her former mother-in-law standing on the wraparound deck of the biggest and most expensive house in Sugar Falls. She didn't know how Bo's biggest fan would react to all the Cooper talk or if Cessy would feel her son's memory was being undermined by Hunter's infatuation with a new male hero. Plus, Hunter had a good point, and she was already feeling like a complete jerk for just abandoning the man like that. "I'll tell you what. You stay here with Gram, and I'll run by the market and then back to the cabin to make sure Cooper's okay."

"I'll go with you." Hunter stayed in his seat even though Cessy was now off the porch and heading to their car.

"No, Gram wants you to show her how to set up her new flat-screen TV. I'll be back in thirty minutes."

After telling Cessy that she forgot something at the market—the less her mother-in-law knew, the better—Maxine drove back toward town. It would take her ten minutes to get up the mountain to Cooper's cabin. That left her with five minutes to get groceries and fifteen minutes to get back to Cessy's in time for her chicken dinner, which seemed to be the only thing her mother-in-law ever cooked on Sunday nights.

She parked in the side lot at Duncan's and grabbed a small metal cart from the rack out front. Normally, she took her time saying hello to her neighbors and friends if she saw them in the store. But she was on a mission this evening and quickly grabbed a loaf of sliced bread, some milk and a few packages of meat and cheese from the deli section. Hmmm. What else would a bachelor marine like? Maybe some cereal or some fresh produce?

Wait, she just wanted to make sure he didn't starve to death. She didn't need to stock his pantry. She headed to the front of the store and passed a heated display case containing fresh roasted chickens.

Maybe he'd like something hot to eat tonight. She *had* been a little snotty earlier, and didn't normally get so defensive. Maybe this would be an olive branch of some sort.

Mauricio Norte was behind the counter and turned to help Maxine just as she'd decided not to waste any more time at the store.

"What can I get you, Miss Maxine?" the older man in the clean white apron asked.

"I'll take one of these chickens please, Mauricio."

"Oh, was there a problem with the one I sold Miss Cessy earlier?"

"Wait." She paused. "You sold a roasted chicken to my mother-in-law today? On Sunday?"

"Yes. We only make the chickens on Sunday, and Miss Cessy buys one every week."

Maxine should've known. For the past three years, the woman had been passing off a store-bought meal as her own. Now she didn't feel so badly for making them hold dinner for her so she could take an arrogant marine some food.

After checking out, she threw the two paper bags into the back of her late model Explorer. She slammed the rear hatch, which crunched on something—probably one of the cereal boxes. Oh, well. A little smashed wheat bran wouldn't hurt him.

She got in her seat and buckled up just as she was pulling out of the lot and onto Snowflake Boulevard. She had fifteen minutes to make it to the cabin and back in time for dinner. Of course, Cessy was probably already giving Hunter the third degree about his pen pal's indefinite stay, and Maxine didn't want any part of that interrogation.

She almost missed the turnoff for the cabin for the second time today, but she slammed on her brakes before it was too late. Her rear tires fishtailed, and she heard the grocery bags topple over. Great. With each divot in the dirt road, the car bounced, causing the groceries to tumble around.

The long gray plume of smoke coming out of the cabin's chimney confirmed what she'd known all along. The man had gotten inside safe and sound and didn't need her or Hunter worrying about him.

But she couldn't go back to Cessy's with a trunk load of spilled groceries. Besides, she really should apologize for her behavior earlier. She got out of the car and opened the rear hatch to assess the damage.

Damn.

It wasn't the box of cereal that had gotten smashed in the rear door. It was the plastic container for the chicken, which had torn free of its compartment and, along with its juices, had slipped and sloshed all over the light upholstery.

Double damn.

She wiped the chicken off as best she could and put it back in the container. Good thing she kept her car fairly clean and vacuumed. It should be safe enough to eat.

The paper bag was leaking chicken juice, but there was nowhere else to put all the groceries. She piled everything back into the two sacks and carried them to the front porch, dribbling juice as she went.

She knocked, balancing the dripping chicken and sandwich fixings in one arm.

No answer.

She could just leave the groceries on the porch. But then Hunter would want to know if she'd apologized to Cooper for the way she'd acted, or he'd want to know if she was sure there were no robbers or zombies looming nearby…

Ugh. She knocked again, this time louder and longer. She kept up the stream of knocking until her knuckles grew numb and she was about to drop the chicken through the juicy tear in the bag.

Suddenly, the door swung open and there he stood, his hair sticking up on the left side of his head, his eyes half-closed. He had a dazed look about him—as if he'd just woken up. And as her gaze dropped to his bare chest, which was phenomenal, with two perfectly rounded pecs tapering down into a set of chiseled abs covered in a dusting of light brown hair, she realized he was only wearing boxer shorts.

He looked warm and sexy and half-aroused. Her first thought was that she wouldn't mind waking up to that every morning. Her second thought was to squeeze her eyes closed and block out the embarrassing realization.

"I…uh…brought you some groceries." She held up the bags just as the chicken tore through the brown paper and landed on the porch, rolling out of the smashed container. The loaf of bread dropped out next.

"Oops." She laughed, self-conscious at her awkwardness. Here she was, standing in front of an almost-naked man and spilling food all over the place.

She would've bent down to pick it up, but his words stopped her.

"You smiled," he said. "At me. Finally."

Again she noted the glazed look in his eyes. Was he still asleep? Maybe he was a sleepwalker. He didn't appear to be angry at her, but he definitely seemed groggy and out of it.

"I smile all the time." She wondered if he even knew who she was.

"I've been waiting for you to smile at me. The whole time I was in the hospital I thought about you. And now you're here." He reached toward her, and his fingers grazed her cheek. "You're so beautiful."

Her heart tumbled as if it had been in the ripped bag with the chicken. She should've backed away, but she couldn't. He had to be talking about another woman and didn't realize she was the wrong person. But as his fingers stroked her cheek, she leaned into the callused warmth. His thumb trailed down to the corner of her mouth, and she clenched her teeth together to keep from kissing it.

The other sack of groceries dropped from her hand, but she let them fall and reached out to hold on to something before she collapsed onto the porch just like everything else. And while the doorjamb might have been a safer bet, she gripped his bare shoulder instead.

She turned her face into his palm, her fingers making the same delicate pattern along his skin.

"You look like an angel when you're not mad at me," he said. "I want you to look at me like that all the time. Like my sweet cookie-queen angel."

His cookie-queen angel? So he *did* know who she was. She really needed to put a stop to this now.

"You smell like your cookies. Do you taste like them?" He pulled her closer. While one hand continued to light her face and lips on fire, his other hand, which held something that appeared to be black steel, reached for her waist.

He lowered his mouth and trailed kisses along her neck. She was going to stop him—really, she was—but when she felt what appeared to be a semiautomatic pistol press against her waist, she finally came to her senses and jerked back. "Wait! Is that a gun?"

"Hmmm?"

Maxine pulled back even more and glanced down at the holstered Glock he held in his hand. The same hand that was pulling her body in closer.

"Why in the world would you come to the door with a gun?"

He smiled. "I'm in a strange house. In a strange city. Never know when a sexy little burglar is going to come by and try to steal my senses."

"Are you drunk?" she asked. There was no way this could be the same man who had been so cold and reserved less than two hours ago.

"Nope. Not if you count one glass of Scotch. But if you add the pain meds… I'm not sure how that works. All I know is that I'm pretty damn relaxed. You want a drink, my cookie angel? I like it when you're not so uptight."

This was crazy. She had to get out of here. "Listen, Cooper. I think you're half-asleep. You need to put the gun down and go back to bed. Hopefully, you won't remember any of this." Even though she would remember every detail. "I'll talk to you later, okay?"

"Okay," he slurred, as she backed away. "Sweet dreams, angel."

Before she lost herself completely, Maxine turned and hurried back to her car. She started the engine and zoomed down the dirt path. When she made it to the main highway, she pulled over and took three deep breaths, just like they'd been taught in Pilates class. Then she took three more.

To hell with Pilates. She needed a glass of wine.

Maxine put her head back against the leather seat and closed her eyes, trying to get her racing heart under control. What had happened back there? She'd completely fallen apart. Panicked.

It wasn't the fact that he had a gun. He was military—and a cop sleeping in a strange place. She should've expected that. Besides, it wasn't as if he'd pulled it on her.

Nor was she upset by the fact that he was so spaced out on painkillers he probably wouldn't remember how she'd softened like warm dough in his hands. Although she still hated the way her body had responded to him.

No, she was upset because even in his medicated state, he'd known exactly who she was—and he'd wanted her.

What made matters even worse was that she'd wanted him, too.

And that reaction upset her most of all.

Who in the hell had trashed his yard?

Cooper first suspected some teenagers had thrown an epic party outside the cabin while he'd been passed out cold inside. A more likely possibility was that an animal—or several—had gotten into a neighbor's trash can and dragged the remains of their picnic across his driveway. Either way, he resolved to cut back on the painkillers—and the Scotch—and to be more on guard when he slept.

Man, he'd had some crazy-ass dreams. All night long, he'd dreamed of Maxine smiling at him. Even when he woke up this morning, he could still smell her vanilla scent and feel the warmth of her smile under his left thumb. Like he said, *crazy*.

After picking up the empty boxes and food wrappers, he decided that if he didn't want tuna again for breakfast, he needed to go into town. It only took three tries to get the engine in the Jeep to turn over, but once it started, the yellow vehicle navigated the mountain roads pretty well. Minutes later, he turned onto Snowflake Boulevard, where the big clock in the center of town read twenty minutes after nine.

He spotted the Sugar Falls Cookie Company and debated parking in front to get some baked goods for breakfast and to check out the enemy camp. But he didn't want to see Maxine in person. It was bad enough he had to see her in his dreams. Instead, he drove another block before parallel parking in front of the Cowgirl Up Café.

The building, which was painted bright purple, looked more like a rodeo bar than a diner. But, when he slammed the car door closed, his mouth watered at the aroma of sizzling bacon and fresh coffee wafting out to the street.

At least the air *used* to smell like bacon. But when he drew closer… What in the world was that stench?

As he walked toward the entrance, where two saddled horses had been tied to a hitching post out front, he spotted a steaming pile of fresh excrement behind a white mare.

Wait. Was he in Idaho or in Texas? And what century was this?

An older man in faded overalls lumbered out of the Cowgirl Up, put a weathered Boise State cap onto his graying head, gave one of the horses a pat on the nose and then got into his once-blue GMC pickup.

Cooper shook his head. Pulling open the café doors, which had been painted to look like the slatted wood entrance to a saloon, he was immediately assaulted with Western motif everywhere the eye could see. Framed pictures of horses adorned the purple-and-pink-striped walls. Miniature cowboy boots—each with a cactus plant growing out of its opening—sat on every table. Behind the counter seating area, someone had tacked up several ropes and looped them together to spell out "Cowgirl Up."

Stirrups and spurs and bridles and other odds and ends one might find in a tack room had been covered in glitter paint and sequins, then nailed to the walls and ceilings.

It looked like a barrel racing rodeo queen had exploded in here. But most of the cowhide-printed booths and wooden chairs and tables were full, so the food must be good.

An older woman with a lime-green apron tied around

her skintight Wrangler jeans nodded her bleached-blond head toward the counter seating. "Have a seat anywhere you want, darlin'. We'll be with you in a hot Tennessee minute."

Cooper had no idea how long a hot Tennessee minute was, but he took the chair along the corner of the counter so he could see everyone who walked in or out.

Some habits were hard to break.

A petite brunette sitting alone at a table directly across from him must've had the same idea because she kept staring at the door. She was pretty in an athletic sort of way, but she sure was skittish. Each time a waitress walked behind her, she started.

He couldn't help watching her for a while, noting that she didn't make eye contact with anyone in the restaurant. Not that Cooper was interested or even attracted to that type, but she looked like a woman with a secret.

And he always liked to find out people's secrets.

The waitress, who could easily pass for Dolly Parton's older, bustier sister, held a steaming pot in front of Cooper's nose. "Can I get you started with some coffee?"

"I'd love some." He turned over his mug. "Thanks."

She put the pot back on the burner behind the counter, then handed him a menu.

Whoa. Those were the longest fingernails he'd ever seen. And they fit right in with the rest of the restaurant's flashy decor.

She placed her hands on her hips, and Cooper tried not to stare at the long magenta-painted tips. Was that a rhinestone on her thumbnail?

"You new in town, or just visiting?"

"Uh, just visiting, ma'am."

"You staying with friends, then?"

Cooper almost choked on his hot coffee. He was used

to being the interrogator, not the other way around, and this dolled up grandma was proving to be quite the small town busybody. "Why would you think I was staying with friends?"

"'Cause if you were staying at Betty Lou's B and B, you wouldn't be eating here right now on account that Betty Lou puts on a good morning spread for her customers. And most of the guests up at the lodge don't come into town for breakfast. So, darlin', seeing as there ain't many other places to stay in Sugar Falls, you must be visiting a friend."

What the woman lacked in fashion sense, she made up for in detective skills.

Cooper avoided responding by asking a question of his own—another habit that was hard to break. "How are the biscuits and gravy, ma'am?"

"Hey, now, none of that *ma'am* business in here." She smiled and pulled out her order pad. "Everyone calls me Freckles. I own the Cowgirl Up and, at the risk of sounding completely biased, the biscuits and gravy are to die for. You want hash browns or home fries with that?"

"Whatever you recommend, Ms. Freckles, and can I get two eggs over easy and a large orange juice with that?"

"Ms. Freckles, huh?" The waitress chuckled and put her pen behind her ear. "I like good manners and big appetites on our visitors. Hope you plan to stick around for a while."

She turned to put his order in before Cooper could tell her that he didn't plan to stay long at all. Hell, he didn't know *what* he planned.

He took another sip of coffee as he surveyed the room. Everyone except the wary brunette looked as if they'd jumped right out of a brochure advertising quaint small towns in America. Not that Cooper had actually spent time in any Main Street USA–type places.

A couple of older men wearing chaps and boots stood up. When their chairs scraped the floor, the skittish woman nearly jumped out of her seat. Yep, there was definitely some type of story going on there.

The taller cowboy placed a tattered and dusty Stetson on his head. "See ya tomorrow, Freckles."

"Wait, Scooter." The café owner rushed over and handed the customer a napkin wrapped bundle. "I packed up some apple slices for you and Jonesy to give Klondike and Blossom."

Cooper assumed that Klondike and Blossom were the two horses outside, but with townspeople named Freckles and Jonesy and Scooter, who knew?

The burly old cowboys thanked the owner and held open the door just as a bundle of blond curls rushed in. Both men stopped in their tracks and dipped their hats.

"Morning, Maxine," the shorter one said.

A warm sensation spread through Cooper's stomach that had nothing to do with the coffee he'd just swallowed and everything to do with the fact that Hunter's mother had just entered the Cowgirl Up Café, looking as sexy as hell in a damp long-sleeved Boise State T-shirt and a short pair of bright blue running shorts. Her legs were just as long, just as tanned and just as tempting as they'd been yesterday. And her top-of-the-line athletic shoes were bright orange and well-worn, indicating she was a legitimate runner.

Just like him.

Dammit. He didn't want to think that he and the beautiful mom had anything in common. It was better they kept their distance. But he couldn't deny that seeing her familiar face in an over-sequin-decorated café filled with nosy strangers was somewhat of a relief.

Maxine waved hello to several of the customers and

said good morning to Freckles before sitting next to the apprehensive brunette and pulling the nervous woman in close for what appeared to be a reassuring hug.

She hadn't noticed him yet, which was just as well. He'd have to say something to her, and he wasn't sure what. He hadn't stopped thinking about her since she and Hunter dropped him off at the cabin last night, which was more than a bit annoying, especially since she'd made it clear he was going to be a pain in her backside—pretty as it was.

Was he going to have to see her every time he came into town? He'd wait until she was done talking to her nervous friend and… What? He wasn't sure what to say, since talking to her was like talking to a prickly cactus.

But the first words she said to her friend pulled him right out of his line of thought.

"So, did the parole board tell you what your options were?"

Chapter Five

"Shh, not so loud." Mia glanced to the left and right, even though Maxine doubted any of the locals were paying a lick of attention to them, then spoke quietly and quickly. "They said that if I want to make sure Nick stays in prison, then I need to come testify in person at the parole hearing. But there's no way I want him to see me. I can't even be in the same room with that asshole. He destroyed my career. He destroyed my life."

Maxine understood her friend and former cheerleading teammate's fear of the man who'd stalked her, and then used a baseball bat to crush both her knee and her dance career. Mia didn't want to have to go through any sort of hearing again, even if there were a thousand prison guards in the room and the psycho was in full handcuffs and restraints. "Can't you just send a letter? Or can someone go on your behalf?"

"They said I could write them or send someone else,

but it won't have the full weight of me giving my own testimony. Hold on—not to change the subject, because I know I can be a little paranoid, but who is that guy over there who keeps staring this way? Do you think Nick sent him to find out where I lived?"

"What guy?" Maxine turned and saw Cooper sitting at the U-shaped counter, digging into a heaping plate of biscuits while watching them with those cold and appraising green eyes. "Crap."

She couldn't believe he was here. She'd hoped to have more time to sort out whatever she was feeling toward him. Instead, her feet itched to run right back out the door.

"Crap, what?" Mia tried to look over Maxine's shoulder.

"Nick didn't send that guy. That's Hunter's pen pal. You know, Gunny Heartthrob?" Maxine kicked herself for the continued use of that nickname.

"Oh." Realization chased the confusion from Mia's expression. "Oh, oh, oh."

Her best friend, who just a few seconds ago had thought every man in the world was out to get her, was now smiling and standing up as if she were going to dance right on over to Cooper and hug him like a long-lost friend.

And since Maxine had made eye contact with him, it wasn't as if she could be totally rude and ignore the guy.

By the time she followed her friend, Mia was already shaking Cooper's hand. "Hi, I'm Hunter's Aunt Mia."

"Ah, the dance teacher. Hunter mentioned you." Cooper put down his fork and reached out his hand to shake Mia's. Then he turned his questioning eyes to Maxine.

"Hi again." Maxine tried to resist the urge to pull her hair loose and run her fingers through it so it didn't look like such a sweaty mess.

"I thought you looked familiar," Mia continued, "but I

didn't know where I recognized you from. But now I realize that it was from all those pictures Maxine showed us when she found them on Hunter's computer—"

Maxine gave her friend a nudge with her elbow, hoping she'd shut up.

"What?" Mia turned to Maxine, letting far more out of the bag than if she'd kept talking. "Why are you looking at me like that?"

Maxine tried to give her friend the international look for shut the heck up, but she wasn't taking the hint.

Mia turned back to the now-grinning man. "Anyway, Hunter's been telling us all about you and your surgery. How do you like Sugar Falls?"

Sweet mercy, he looked good when he wasn't glaring at her. She'd noticed his smile several times yesterday on their drive home from the hospital. But it had only been directed at Hunter. That was, until last night, when she'd gone back to the cabin and he'd turned it on her. Now he'd aimed it at Mia, and Maxine wasn't sure she liked it.

"I'm still trying to figure that out," he replied. "The Gregson cabin is pretty quiet and it's a lot less rustic than I was expecting. This is my first venture into town. It's definitely different from anything I'm used to."

What was he trying to say? That their town was Podunk? That it didn't live up to his big-city standards? Well, maybe he should pack up his cute marine butt and leave.

"I know," Mia said, turning traitor. "When I got here from Miami, it was like night and day for me. At least I'd lived in Boise while we were in college. But small town life grows on you, and now I just love it here. Everyone looks out for each other and strangers stick out like sore thumbs."

"Yeah, well this sore thumb is definitely feeling out of

place." This time, he included Maxine in his shy smile, and her heart rate slipped into overdrive, beating faster than it had an hour ago when she was sprinting back into town after getting Mia's 9-1-1 text.

"You'll get used to it. Have Max introduce you around town. Then she can take you up to the waterfalls and show you where all the local hot spots are."

"Whoa, Mia. Pump your brakes." When did it become Maxine's responsibility to introduce the guy to everyone and play tour guide? "Cooper is just here to recover from his surgery. I'm sure he doesn't want us bothering him with all the touristy things."

And Gunny Heartthrob's glare was back. What'd she say? She was sure he would have wanted to say the same thing himself.

At that, Mia finally seemed to catch the vibe between the two of them and said, "Um, it was nice meeting you, but I have that mommy-and-me ballet class starting in a few minutes, so I gotta…"

Her friend walked out of the café without finishing her goodbye, but apparently Cooper hadn't noticed because he didn't take his eyes off Maxine.

"Hey there, Max," Freckles called out from where they'd been previously sitting before Mia did her Bambi in the headlights impersonation and ran out. "If you and Mia don't need this table anymore, can the boys from the Kiwanis Club grab it for their meeting? I'll bring your farmer's scramble over to that side of the counter and you can eat with your friend."

All the other diners swiveled their heads toward them, and Maxine didn't know how to get out of making a scene. She slowly sank into the counter seat next to the man and bit her tongue to keep from apologizing for the obvious awkwardness.

"Are you going to drink that?" She reached for the frosty glass of fresh orange juice in front of him and drained it before he could object. She needed to cool down her emotions and her nerves. And maybe even her hormones.

"So what's up with your friend?" he asked.

"Mia?" Sharp prickles of jealousy set her already-strained nerves on edge. "She's single, if that's what you're asking, but she definitely isn't looking."

"No!" He sounded offended. "I'm not asking… I mean, I'm not interested in… She's not my type… I mean, I'm not looking, either."

So he had a type, but he wasn't looking for a relationship. The man was a complete enigma.

"What I'm trying to ask is why does she look like she's terrified of her own shadow?"

"Oh, that. She's not usually so jittery." Actually, jittery was an understatement, but Maxine didn't want him to think there was anything wrong with her friend. It was bad enough that he'd already reverted back to his macho attitude and his annoyance at her. He didn't need any more fuel to add to his testosterone fire. "She had a really bad stalker situation a couple of years before she moved here."

"That's rough," he conceded, taking her by surprise. "What are the local police doing about it?"

"Oh, we don't have a local police force. At least, not yet. But with all the increased tourism, the city council recently voted to establish a small-ish department."

"How small-ish?"

She could see the wheels turning behind those constantly appraising eyes, and she needed to throw a wrench in his mental gears before he got any ideas about continuing his policing career in Sugar Falls.

"Super small-ish. Tiny. In the last town council meeting, I think they said the entire force would consist of a police chief and maybe a couple of officers. Right now the city contracts all their law enforcement needs to the county sheriff's office, who would still handle all the big stuff. So, yeah, boring and small-ish."

"Yeah, you said that."

Ugh, the man was so patronizing. But before she could shoot him a withering look, Freckles put a plate of scrambled eggs tossed with fresh vegetables in front of her and refilled the empty orange juice glass.

"Thank you," she managed to get out before the café owner raised an eyebrow at the obvious tension radiating between them.

"So does the sheriff know about the stalker?" Cooper asked as he resumed eating what appeared to be biscuits underneath the now-congealed plate of gravy.

Apparently, he'd set his plate aside when she sat down and had been waiting for her to be served. The man might be arrogant and patronizing, but at least he had good manners—even if he still hadn't thanked her for the groceries. In fact, he was acting as if last night at the cabin had never even happened. Well, two could play that game.

"No. Mia doesn't want anyone to know her business. She's really private like that. Besides, the guy is in prison as of today, so there isn't any real threat. Yet."

"As of today? Yet? Is that why she's so jumpy? She's expecting something to happen?"

Maxine didn't want to betray her friend's confidence, but Cooper had a background in law enforcement. Maybe he could advise them on how to keep the psycho away. "Nick Galveston—that's the stalker—is up for a parole hearing. That's why Mia's all worked up. Not that I blame her. He's a real scary dude. Crazy scary."

"Crazy is the worst kind of scary because you never

know what they're going to do. She really needs to advise the local sheriff so they're aware of the situation."

"Ha, like that would help. I don't think Mia places much stock in an overburdened sheriff's department with a bunch of men who barely graduated high school running things. She doesn't really trust the good ole boy network. No offense."

"None taken, since I'm not a good ole boy."

He definitely wasn't, she had to agree. There was nothing good and nothing boy about the way he was looking her up and down right that second.

The sweat from her T-shirt clung to her back, and she knew her sports bra wasn't confining her breasts as well as it should. But did he have to be so obvious in the way he was staring at her?

And did her cheeks have to burn with the realization that he was still finding her attractive, even though he was no longer under the influence of his pain pills?

She needed to change the subject. "So, uh, Hunter asked me if he could ride his bike out to your cabin after school, even though he knows I won't let him ride down the highway by himself. I figured you and I should probably talk and lay out some ground rules."

Cooper leaned back in his seat, his tanned palms rubbing along the sides of his jeans. Was he agitated?

"Some ground rules for what?" He crumbled the paper napkin in his lap and squeezed it tightly.

Yep, she'd definitely offended him again. But Hunter was her baby. She didn't care who she pissed off as long as she kept her son safe.

"Look, I'm sure you're a really nice guy and that you mean well, but Hunter doesn't have a father figure or a male role model or anything. And for whatever reason, he's looking to you to fill that position. But he's an impressionable little boy and I don't know you from Adam. I don't want Hunter getting his expectations up and then getting hurt."

"And you think I'm going to hurt him?"

"I don't know what you'll do or why you'll do it. I don't even know why you're here." She took another drink of his juice before forcing a smile at Freckles and the Kiwanis Club members, who'd begun to eye her and Cooper with obvious interest.

"Listen, lady, I don't know why I'm here, either. Maybe because I didn't have anywhere else to go when I got out of the Corps. Or maybe because I bonded with a ten-year-old boy who seems to need me. I never knew my dad and my mom died when I was twelve. I don't have much experience with kids or with parental figures. But this is obviously an issue for you, and the last thing I want to do is cause a problem between you and your son. So let Hunter know I had to leave town sooner than expected, and I won't write him anymore."

Maxine tried not to let the sudden sympathy she felt show on her face. A proud man like Cooper wouldn't welcome it. So she sat there silently as he opened his fist and emptied the rumpled paper contents onto the table. The napkin was now in shreds, just as Hunter's heart would be if he found out his mom made Cooper leave without saying goodbye. Before she could stop herself, she reached out and placed her fingers over the top of his.

"No, that's not what I want." His hand stilled beneath her palm. The heat radiated off his skin, and she kept her fingers in place, waiting for him to make eye contact or otherwise reassure her that he wasn't going to leave.

He did neither. But he also didn't pull away.

Geez, she'd been secretly willing him to get out of town

since yesterday afternoon, but now she was practically begging him to stay. She needed to make up her mind.

"I think we got off on the wrong foot," she continued. "I'm not opposed to you being here or to you having a relationship with my son. I'm smart enough to know that Hunter has changed for the better since he's been talking to you. He's not so insecure and he's been doing better with the other kids at school. I'm just worried because he can make a really big deal out of things, and in his eyes, you're the biggest deal yet. He's put you on this pedestal and I guess I'm worried that you're going to get bored with him and break his heart."

Just as his dad got bored with both of them and broke their hearts.

"I don't get it, either." He glanced at the shredded napkin and their joined hands. When their gazes met again, her heart stopped for a beat. "But for some reason Hunter and I have bonded. And believe me, I'm not the bonding sort. Nor am I the pedestal sort. But I can promise you that I'm not going to get bored with him. I don't see how anyone could get bored around that kid."

That scored him a few points because Maxine felt the exact same way about her only child.

"Besides, once he realizes that I'm just some regular guy with a bum knee and no job, he'll probably lose interest and be happy to see me go on my way."

Maxine didn't know when it'd happened, but Cooper's hand had turned over and she was holding it. Her heart had turned over, too, and she was at risk of passing it over to a stranger who seemed just as lonely and as insecure as Hunter.

Whoa.

She didn't need that. She lifted her hand from his and picked up her fork, trying to be as nonchalant as she could about the fact that she'd been touching him so intimately. Just as he'd done to her last night, although he still hadn't brought it up. She could only hope he'd been so loopy that he didn't remember it.

"So then you'll stay?" she asked, forcing her mouth to chew the eggs she'd just lost her appetite for.

"If you're sure it won't cause any problems."

The only problem she was immediately aware of was that she was becoming more and more attracted to him, which she'd die before admitting to anyone.

"No, but you'll have to tell me if at any point Hunter starts overwhelming you. I don't want you feeling obligated to hang out with him all the time."

"Deal. So are you cool with him hanging out with me after school?"

"Uh, actually, that's kind of a long way for him to ride. And I usually don't let him take his bike on the street when he's by himself—"

His gaze intensified to the point she could hardly breathe, let alone think or speak. And as the corners of his lips quirked up in a sly grin, she put her fork on her plate, sat back in her chair and crossed her arms. "Why are you smirking like that?"

"I didn't mean riding his bike along the highway. I could pick him up. So, are you worried about him having a relationship with me? Or are you just being a little overprotective about his safety with me?"

"Overprotective?" Was he pointing out her parenting flaws again?

It was a good thing she'd put her fork down, because if she hadn't, she might've used it to stab him in the hand she'd been stroking earlier. It would've been a shame because they were such warm and strong hands. Too bad they were attached to such a macho jerk.

"Relax," he said. "Don't get in such a huff, Mama Bear. There's nothing wrong with looking out for your little cub. He's your kid and I'm not here to undermine you or challenge all these rules you've given him—but just between you and me, you *do* realize that someday you're going to have to let him grow up, right?"

"Great." Maxine lifted the orange juice glass in a mock toast. "I'm getting parenting advice from a single marine who's never had a child, has spent the last year living in a tent in the desert and walks around looped up on pain meds, answering the door with a gun in his hand."

His brows drew together in puzzlement before a blank expression covered his face. Yep. He for sure didn't remember last night, but he apparently was too proud to admit it.

He lifted his coffee mug and returned her sarcastic toast. "Well, I know a *lot* about being a little boy and being forced to grow up."

"Yeah, and I know a lot about being a parent and about being a woman, so let me give *you* a little piece of advice. Telling a female to relax has the exact opposite effect you probably intended."

She would've thrown some money on the counter to pay for her meal before making a grand exit, but she had come here directly from her run and was only carrying her smartphone and earbuds. She stood and turned toward the exit anyway, intent on settling up with Freckles later today.

But before she could get to the door, she heard Cooper call out, "So don't worry yourself then. I'll just pick up Hunter after school and bring him home."

She let the painted saloon door slam behind her, not willing to acknowledge his parting shot with a response.

Don't worry yourself, he'd said. First he'd told her to

relax and then not to worry. Why was he deliberately trying to annoy her?

She'd had a brief moment of understanding toward the man, but then they'd come full circle and now she was annoyed as hell with him all over again. And what made it worse, was that he seemed to enjoy getting her all flustered.

She jogged across the street, back toward the cookie shop. The only thing she *wouldn't* worry about was the fact that she planned to ignore him like crazy when he brought Hunter home this afternoon.

To: matthewcooper@usmc.mil
From: hunterlovestherockies@hotmail.net
Re: Best Day of My Life
Date: March 14
I can't believe that your really here in Sugar Falls. Jake Marconi is gonna freak out when you pick me up at school. His dad owns the Gas N'Mart and Jake gets to go there after school and have all the candy and slushies he wants. He said all the other kids go there for snacks after school whenever there dads pick them up and he sells them junk while the dads talk about camping and football and stuff. Now that your here, I can go also. It will be so sweet. Specially cause you are way more cooler then boring old Mr. Marconi.
From Hunter
p.s. I can't wait.
p.s.s. My mom said your really nice and she doesn't care if we hang out all the time and do cool guy stuff together.
p.s.s.s. Make sure to give me your new local email address cause you probly can't keep the military one no more.

She needed to talk to Hunter about leaving his computer in the living room and switched on all the time. Yet, her electricity bill was the least of her worries.

She'd barely glanced at the open email on the screen before powering off the laptop. She wanted no reminders of the man who'd parked his bright yellow four-by-four man-machine down the street and left it there all morning as he limped around to several shops downtown. To make matters worse, she'd never told Hunter that she thought Cooper was nice or that they could hang out all the time.

Still, it broke her heart that Hunter thought he needed a man to pick him up from school just so he could fit in with the other boys who had dads. She wanted to drive to Marconi's Gas N'Mart and dump a bag of Doritos in the slushy machine just to spite all the mean classmates who left her son out of all the "cool kid" activities. But it wasn't Jake Marconi's fault that Bo died. Or that Hunter had now latched on to a good-looking, smart-mouthed pen pal who set her senses on high alert just by parking his borrowed vehicle in the same vicinity as her apartment.

Her home telephone rang, and when she saw the name on the caller ID, she hesitated. She didn't want to answer Cessy's call, but if she didn't, she'd just spend the rest of the morning staring out her second-floor window, shooting daggers at the man who had sent her whole world spinning.

Maxine chose the lesser of two evils. "Hi, Cessy."

"So now that Hunter's at school, we can talk freely. Tell me what you thought."

"Thought of what?"

"Don't play coy, Maxine. What did you think of that Matthew Cooper guy? Hunter hasn't been able to stop talking about him for weeks. But now that he's in town, you've been acting even tenser than you usually do. Are you distraught about their relationship? Are you worried that he might replace Bo in Hunter's heart?"

No, Maxine wasn't worried about that since Bo had really never had the opportunity to lodge himself in the boy's heart before overindulging in a cocktail-infused lunch and driving off the road. But she wasn't going to say as much to her mother-in-law.

"Mr. Cooper seems nice enough," she said instead. "But I don't really know much about him other than he was in the Marines." Plus the fact that he'd lost his mom when he was barely older than Hunter, and he'd basically never had a father. But Maxine didn't want to share that personal revelation.

"I had one of my people over at town hall do a computer check on him."

Sweet mercy. When Cessy said "one of her people," she meant someone who owed her a favor. Without a doubt, the woman had no shame when it came to wheedling some poor government employee into running a background search on a complete stranger.

"Cessy, that's probably illegal and definitely unethical. Not to mention a complete infringement on Mr. Cooper's privacy." Um. Yeah. So said the woman who'd just read her son's open email. But that was different. She really didn't think Hunter would care. And if he did care, then he needed to stop leaving his personal correspondence out in the open for the entire world to see.

"You want to know what I found out or not?" Cessy asked.

Maxine rubbed her temples as she walked away from her living room window and dropped onto her sofa. She hated to encourage the woman's antics, but she was dying to know. And tempted to grab a pad of paper and take notes.

"I guess," she said, trying to maintain a disinterested tone.

"He's actually on the up-and-up. Distinguished military record, lots of medals and awards, great investigator, yada, yada, yada. He doesn't own any property, but his credit's good. We were limited in what we could find out about his exact finances, but if we want to, we can call Phil Hemingway over at the bank."

"No, Cessy! Do *not* call anyone at the bank to snoop into the man's—"

"Let's see what else," the woman continued, as though she hadn't heard any protest. "He's from Detroit originally. Foster kid. Not sure about what happened to his family but he doesn't have children of his own. Appears he's been married before, but according to what Mary Pat…uh, I mean…my source, could find out, it couldn't have been longer than a few months. Looks like the ex is remarried now with a couple kids, so he doesn't seem to have any romantic entanglements."

Maxine zeroed in on the mention of Cooper being divorced. She wondered what Cooper's former wife was like. And who was to blame for the marriage going sour so quickly. Then something clicked, and it dawned on her that her mother-in-law was purposely pointing out an attractive man's marital status.

"Why would I be interested in the guy's love life or his inability to keep a woman?" Wow, did that come out sounding defensive or what? But it was too late to retract the snide—and untrue—remark.

"Of course you wouldn't be interested. That'd be totally inappropriate and unseemly, dear." Cessy made a tsk sound. "Besides, even if you *could* get a guy like him to fall for little ole you, it wouldn't be anything like what you and Bo shared. Something like that only comes around once in a lifetime."

Normally, Cessy's comments painting her son as something he most definitely was not would roll right off Maxine's back. But the curls along her neckline bristled and her spine straightened at the implication that she couldn't land a man like Cooper. Granted, he'd been under the influence of something last night, but she was pretty sure that if she would've let him have his way, she could've sealed the deal.

Which was why she needed to make sure the man never got his way. And the only strategy she could come up with was to ignore him completely or stay the heck away from him.

Because so far, Maxine's resistance to the growing mutual attraction between her and Gunny Heartthrob was about as dependable as a wet paper bag from Duncan's Market.

As Cooper drove back to the cabin before two o'clock, he went over every word Maxine had said to him in the café. He understood some of her concern, but he didn't get her hostile attitude toward him in particular. Hunter had never said as much, but Cooper got the feeling there was no love lost between Maxine and her dead husband. But did that mean she had to take out her relationship issues on him?

Plus, what was that comment she'd made about him being doped up on pain meds and answering the door with a gun?

Although, he *had* been pretty out of it last night. And he sort of remembered being asleep and hearing a knock on the door, but if he had gotten out of bed, he would've seen whoever or whatever had left all that trash in his front yard.

He pulled into the driveway and parked the Jeep behind the cabin before he unloaded the bat and baseball gloves he bought at Russell's Sports and the groceries he'd stocked up on while he'd been in town. He had a couple hours before Hunter got out of school and he wanted to do a little research on his computer.

Luckily, the cabin was up-to-date on its twenty-first-century technology and had internet access and a landline so he could make a few phone calls.

Alex Russell, the guy who owned the sporting goods store, told him that cell phone reception was spotty up in Sugar Falls, but Cooper still planned to get a smartphone when he went into Boise later this week.

Alex had also told him about Little League season starting this weekend, and Cooper was determined to have Hunter try out for a team. Of course, he wasn't used to dealing with such a hardheaded mom and didn't know how to go about it just yet.

So in the meantime, he'd focus on what he *did* know how to deal with. Investigations. He started with a basic Google search and typed in the name Maxine had mentioned and the city where Mia said she'd moved from.

Boom. There he was, Nick Galveston, a second-string professional football punter who was currently serving a ten-year sentence for terrorist threats, assault and battery, and attempted murder.

His pulse quickened, just as it had whenever he'd found a new lead in a case. Man, he was missing his job already.

He scrolled through some old news articles until he could piece together what had happened to Maxine's friend. It looked as if Mia had been a professional cheerleader when the team's punter took an unhealthy interest in her. The jerk must've had a problem understanding that no meant *no,* and her rejection of his advances turned into a nightmarish stalking situation that ended up with him attacking Mia with a baseball bat.

No wonder the lady was afraid of her own shadow. Nobody should have to live like that.

His own reconstructed leg tightened to an ache, and he sympathized with the poor woman. Just like him, some jackass with a vendetta ruined a perfectly good career and screwed up someone's life. Unlike him, though, it looked like Mia had moved on and put the pieces of her life back together in Sugar Falls.

But, of course, she had someone like Maxine looking out for her. If Cooper had a protective friend on his side, he could probably put a lot behind him, too.

He picked up the white corded phone in the kitchen and dialed the number of a former MP he'd been stationed with at Guantanamo Bay.

After the third ring, a voice finally answered. "Chris Sanchez, Florida Department of Corrections."

"Corporal Sanchez, it's Gunny Cooper." Cooper cringed, knowing he no longer held the rank of gunnery sergeant. Hell, he no longer held the rank of anything. But he didn't know how to define himself now.

"Coop, how the hell are you?" asked the only man to have ever beat him in the Gitmo MP's pull-up contest.

The buddies made small talk before Cooper finally got to the reason for his call. "So, anyway, I hear you have an inmate up for parole over there, and I need a favor."

"Gunny, you know I owe you way more than a favor. I don't have too much pull with the parole board, but there are a few devil dogs who do the local hearings. What do you need?"

As he filled Chris Sanchez in on Mia's situation, he told himself he was trying to help a scared woman who, like him, had been a victim of some sociopath's warped mind. Cooper was one of the good guys and a seeker of justice. But he wasn't above scoring some points by helping out the friend of his sexy cookie angel.

Angel?

Why in the world would he think of her like that? There hadn't been anything angelic about Maxine Walker this morning when she'd gone a couple of rounds with him for wanting to hang out with Hunter.

Unfortunately, he found himself liking it when she threw her halo into the verbal sparring ring.

Chapter Six

That evening, Cooper pulled the Jeep into the rear of the bakery. He would've rather parked out front, but Hunter assured him this was where all their guests parked. He didn't think the boy's mom would agree with the assessment of him being a guest. More like persona non grata.

After school, he'd taken Hunter to the Little League field and the new bat and mitts had been a huge hit. Cooper's knee was pretty much blown after the hour they'd spent throwing the ball back and forth and from all the pitches he'd made to the overly excited kid, so he was anxious to get back to the cabin to elevate and ice it.

When he'd been Hunter's age, he'd walked all over his neighborhood in Detroit, which was light-years removed from Sugar Falls. He knew the kid could let himself into the bakery and would be safe if Cooper just drove off. But Maxine would probably raise hell if he didn't baby her little boy the same way she did.

Besides, he liked seeing her all riled. Maybe, if he was in luck, she had yet to calm down from their earlier confrontation at the Cowgirl Up.

"Mom, we're home." Hunter raced up the back stairs, swinging his backpack around wildly. "I had the best time ever. Tomorrow, Coop's gonna take me back to the cabin, and we're gonna try to catch some fish from the stream. He said it feeds all the way into the Sugar River."

Cooper's worn-out knee could barely get him up the stairs, forcing him to take one step at a time as he gingerly followed his ten-year-old friend.

On second thought, he might not be physically ready for round two with the woman he'd spent all night dreaming about.

"Hi, sweetie. I'm glad you guys had fun." Maxine hugged her son, and then ran her hand through his hair. She then scanned every square inch of the boy, as if checking him for damage. "But maybe we should skip tomorrow so you don't wear Cooper out."

There she went with that overprotective bossiness. Was she suggesting that he was too weak to handle it?

"Nah, he can't wear me out." Cooper looked around the spacious apartment that boasted an open floor plan consisting of a white and stainless steel kitchen that was twice as big as the cozy living room it overlooked. He assumed the two-member family spent a lot of time in or around the kitchen, which made sense as he assumed the woman enjoyed cooking and baking. "Besides, that's why I'm in Sugar Falls—to spend time with my favorite pen pal."

When he high-fived the boy, Maxine rolled her eyes.

She'd obviously showered from her earlier run and had changed into a tight pair of low-waisted white jeans and the same boots she'd worn when she'd picked him up at the airport and then the hospital. She also had on a white sweater that clung to every curve she had up top. She must really have a thing for the color white. And with her golden curls flowing loosely around her head in a halo effect, it was no wonder he kept thinking she looked like an angel.

Too bad her eyes were shooting nonangelic daggers at him.

"Hey, Coop, come check out my room. You can see the Lego set I'm working on." Hunter dropped his backpack and took off down the hallway.

Cooper raised a brow at Maxine, as if to get permission to enter their family sanctuary. He didn't mind riling her up, but he didn't want to be an ill-mannered jerk in someone else's home. And he'd meant it when he said he didn't want to cross any boundaries that would undermine her role as Hunter's parent and primary authority figure.

She extended her arm in a "be my guest" gesture, yet she turned back toward the kitchen, clearly not intent on partaking in the tour. As he followed Hunter, he noted that their home was decorated in various shades of white, with some white highlights and a splash of white thrown in for good measure. Yep, the woman certainly had a thing for the bland color.

At least the floors and accent tables were a deep, dark wood to give some contrast. Plus, all the pillows and throw blankets scattered around contained different textures and fabrics, which layered over each other and looked anything but bland. This apartment was definitely refurbished and definitely expensive. But it also gave off a homey and special vibe—not that he'd experienced that vibe before.

What Cooper would've given to have a house like this when he was growing up… Hunter was a lucky kid. A talkative kid, but a lucky one.

The boy chattered nonstop for the next ten minutes, showing him every single toy and treasure crammed into his oversize, but organized, bedroom. This seemed to be the only room in the apartment with a mishmash of colors, and he was glad Maxine at least allowed her son to be himself when it came to decorating his personal space.

His investigator's eye picked up every detail, and he couldn't help but notice the only thing lacking in Hunter's room was any type of trophies or awards. It was a shame because a great kid like him deserved to have some tangible accolades.

"And that's my mom's room across the hall." Hunter pointed his chubby arm. "It's way bigger than mine, even though I have, like, twice the stuff she has. But that's okay, because she lets me hang out in there with her anytime I want. Even when her friends are over and they're doing their girl talk."

There were two frames on her dresser—one containing a picture of Hunter when he was a toddler, the other a shot of Maxine, Mia and Kylie in blue-and-orange cheerleader outfits. Cooper felt like a voyeur staring into her bedroom and taking in the painted wrought-iron bed and crisp bedding that had to have cost at least a couple hundred dollars. Of course it was white, but for some reason, it also looked warm. And comforting. Cooper could see why anyone would want to spend time in there—even if it meant listening to girl talk.

"My mom worries that I hear too much, but Aunt Kylie says it's good for me to learn all about how to understand a woman and treat her right so I don't end up being a nogood tool like some of the other men they know."

What Cooper wanted to tell the kid was that he should run for the hills whenever he saw a gaggle of women get together for a man-bashing session. But he figured Hunter would learn that for himself soon enough. Besides, what Cooper wouldn't have given to be able to climb up into his own mom's bed and have a conversation with her. But Linda Cooper hadn't been much of a talker before she'd died and her jackass of a husband had kept her from having many female friends. "Have you picked up any good advice?"

"Well, my mom said the way to sweep a woman off her feet is to be secure in who I am and to not try and be something I'm not. Aunt Kylie says I need to always treat a girl like she's a lady and she's the most important thing in my life. Aunt Mia said I need to know when a girl isn't interested in me and move on. But I'm pretty sure Kayla Patrelli might be interested in me. At least, when I wrote her that poem she didn't call me Chubba Bubba like some of the other kids do."

Cooper was at a loss because it sounded as if Hunter at age ten knew a whole lot more about females than he did at age thirty-four. "I guess that's pretty promising."

His knee was screaming for an ice pack, so he cut the awkward hallway conversation about budding romances short by heading back the way they'd come.

Maxine was standing behind the kitchen counter, her hand shoved into a bag of sour cream and onion flavored potato chips and a glass of white wine sitting next to her that Cooper could've sworn she hadn't had when he first got here. Did he drive the woman to drink?

"So I'll see you tomorrow after school," he told Hunter, trying to make a quick exit.

"Wait, my mom is making chicken and rice casserole for dinner. You wanna stay? She's a real good cook."

Maxine's eyes grew wide, and she tried to subtly shake her head at her son, but the poor boy didn't take any notice. His eager stare was glued to Cooper.

"Actually, I just bought a ton of groceries today and was going to do some cooking of my own."

"Why did you buy groceries today? You didn't like the stuff my mom got you from the market yesterday?"

Maxine shoved another chip in her mouth and turned back toward the oven, as if she was too busy to partake in their conversation.

"What groc…?" Cooper started to ask when he remembered the mess of litter on the lawn. "Wait, did you come by last night?"

Without looking back at him, Maxine guzzled down the rest of her liquid fortification and stirred something in a pot on her stove. Yet, all the burners were off. She nodded as if whatever she had in that cold pot was more important than a polite reply. So why wouldn't she look him in the eyes?

"I thought I heard a knocking, but I'd just taken some pain meds and I must've gone back to sleep. Why did you just leave the food on the porch? When I came outside this morning, there were trash and food wrappers all over the yard."

"You didn't go back to sleep." She kept stirring whatever she was pretending to cook. "You opened the door. You saw me holding the bags. You even, uh… I don't know why you didn't take them inside after I left." She looked at her empty glass as if contemplating a refill, but must have decided against it.

Was that what she meant by her earlier comment about him answering the door with his gun? Did he pull a gun on her and scare her?

"Did…uh…anything else happen?" Man, he wanted to just come out and ask her what in the hell she was trying to avoid telling him, but he was afraid of what her answer would be. Maybe it was better to drop the conversation. It was his modus operandi when things got too personal.

Her head swiveled toward Hunter before finally gazing at Cooper. She looked at him the same way her friend Mia had back at the café. Like she was nervous as hell. But she obviously wasn't afraid of Cooper, otherwise she wouldn't let her precious child hang out with him. So why was she in such a panic?

"Nope. Nothing at all." She answered too quickly, then went back to stirring. "Hunter, it's time for homework. Cooper, Hunter can show you out. Enjoy your fresh groceries."

And with that awkward dismissal, he limped down the steps and outside.

As he powered the Jeep to life, he couldn't help but wonder what exactly had happened when he answered the door last evening. And if that was the reason he'd spent the rest of the night tossing and turning.

Something told him it was—and that he'd have to make things right with her. The problem was, he didn't know where to start.

Hunter Walker: Hey Coop. This is my cell phone number so you can store it in your new phone.

Cooper: I'm sitting right next to you, Hunter. You could have just told me.

Hunter Walker: I know. But I'm still practicing with the new phone Gram bought me. My mom thinks I'm too young to have a iPhone but Gram doesnt always listen to my mom. Hey, you want to go out to dinner with me and Gram tonight?

Cooper: Will that be okay with your mom?

Hunter Walker: She wont care. Tonite is her nite to go out and talk about lame girl stuff with her freinds.

Hunter Walker: We R going 2 Patrelli's 4 dinner n Kayla
will B there. Member I told U about her.

Cooper: I'm only going to type this once, so make sure
you read this carefully. If you text me in code like that
again, I will NOT write back. Now, when you see Kayla...

"So I'm wearing my new dress, the black one with silver sequins and my silver Jimmy Choo sling backs, and
he pulls into this church parking lot."

"On your first date?" Maxine asked Kylie.

The curvy redhead had a new date every week, and
her stories always involved trendy clothes and a man
doing something horribly wrong. Maxine didn't know
where her former team-cocaptain-turned-CPA found
these guys.

She tried to pay attention to the story, but she couldn't
get her mind off Cooper. Heck, if she was honest, she
hadn't been able to get her mind off him this whole week.
Of course, it didn't help that her car still smelled like
roasted chicken, which only served to remind her of that
night she'd gone back to the cabin. Thankfully, he didn't
seem to recall anything about it. Although, it wouldn't
have bothered her if she'd been a bit more memorable.

At least he'd been a perfect gentleman since then. He'd
picked up Hunter from school every day this week. And
while he normally brought her son home before the evening meal, tonight Hunter had talked him into going out
with Cessy for their Thursday-night dinner.

"What kind of church?" Mia asked, bringing Maxine
back to the conversation.

"Does it matter what kind?" Maxine lowered herself
into a plank position. Their Pilates instructor was throwing them some pretty nasty looks and often had to remind

the three single women to maintain the focus of the class. In other words, to hush up.

"Well, I was just curious…" Mia said, probably because their friend wasn't even a nonactive member of the community church. "Remember when Kylie had that date with the missionary and he showed up on his bike with his short-sleeved white shirt and name tag?"

"I met him when we were on a white-water rafting trip," Kylie said, defending herself. "He didn't look that religious when he was wearing swim trunks and a life vest. Anyway, back to last night. I never got inside because when we got there, I asked him what kind of restaurant is in a church basement. He said it wasn't a restaurant. They were having a potluck supper for his church's couples counseling group."

Maxine lost her pose and plopped down on her mat, laughing hysterically.

"Ladies, we're focusing here." Mia breathed deeply to cover up her giggling smirk.

"So how did the potluck go?" Maxine asked.

"I'm sure it went just fine, but I wouldn't know because I walked home. I wasn't going into that place. Who the heck would take someone there on a first date?"

"Listen, Kylie." Mia stretched her feet off the mat and onto the hardwood floor. "I'm starting to think there's something off with your picker."

"You're just *now* starting to think that?" Maxine looked at the quiet brunette incredulously. "There's been something off with her picker since we all lived in the dorms."

"I'm so glad that I can share my miserable dating experiences with you two and you don't judge me." Kylie rolled her eyes. "Max, Bo has been dead for eight years now. When are you going to stop judging my bad dates and start going out with some of your own?"

"Never," Maxine responded. "I'm done with men. And their egos."

"Well, I ran into Hunter and Gunny Heartthrob over at Russell Sports. I wouldn't be too done with *him* if I were you."

"Oh, I'm more than done with that one. Done with a capital D-O-N-E." Maxine hoped she sounded halfway convincing.

"Really? I got a good feeling from him," Mia chimed in with a hushed whisper. "And you guys know I never get good feelings about guys. Ever."

"You two women are the most anti-male friends I have," Kylie complained. "Something is seriously wrong with both of you. Mia, you're still running from men, and Maxine can't be bothered either way. Don't you guys miss the excitement, the romance?"

"How exciting and romantic was the church potluck?" Maxine countered.

"Not as exciting as the garlic knots I'm about to order when we get out of class. I've been thinking about dinner at Patrelli's all day."

Maxine's stomach chose that exact moment to growl at the mention of hot buttery bread bits smothered in garlic and parmesan cheese. She'd skipped lunch to go over her invoices, and then had to help Hunter practice his spelling test before his Gram picked him up. Lord knew she couldn't count on Cessy to make her son do any homework. And it was anyone's guess how late they'd be out tonight having dinner with Cooper. Poor guy. He had no idea what he'd gotten himself into when he'd accepted their invitation.

Maxine pushed on her empty stomach, hoping the growling would obey the annoyed instructor, as well. She stared at herself in the mirrored wall as she stretched. Her long and athletic legs were still her best feature, but she was starting to see the hints of age. Her body was still the compact version reminiscent of her cheerleading days, but her blue eyes were more tired and her face a bit more tense. She definitely needed to kick up her skin regime. And maybe do a hot oil treatment on her overly curly blond hair. Bird's nest didn't even begin to describe her style, and that was on a *good* day.

She tried not to compare herself to her friends in the mirror as they did their final deep breathing exercises. Kylie was shaped like a comic book heroine—strong with lots of curves and a teeny-tiny waist. Mia had the slim and graceful lines of a svelte dancer. And there she was—stuck somewhere in the middle.

Kylie had her mat rolled up and was heading to the door, cutting Maxine's self-recriminations short. "Move it, girls. Those carbs aren't going to eat themselves."

Screw the carbs. It was girls' night, after all, and Maxine wanted a glass of merlot. And a straw. Especially if she had to hear about Gunny Heartthrob any more tonight.

The women, still dressed in their workout clothes, made their way one block down Snowflake Boulevard—the main street to end all Main Streets. Maxine had fallen in love with this town when she'd moved here with Bo at the young and impressionable age of twenty-two. She'd been pregnant and wanted to settle down in a small town and raise a family. As a military brat who'd had to relocate all her life, she knew she'd never move again the moment she first laid eyes on the Victorian storefronts that lined the quaint streets.

As Mia opened the large oak door of Patrelli's Italian Restaurant, the aroma of garlic and yeast assaulted Maxine's senses, making her light-headed. She recognized their hostess, a girl in Hunter's class. Kayla Patrelli was pretty, with short and glossy dark hair and big brown doe eyes. She seemed way too young to be working, but she efficiently sat the women at their favorite red vinyl booth in the back corner and passed out plastic-covered menus.

Maybe Maxine should make Hunter work in the cookie shop. She had to do something with him. He didn't seem to be interested in anything other than computer games and baseball. The pediatrician had warned her to limit his screen time, but she worried about him getting involved in organized sports, only to get disappointed if he couldn't live up to his dad's reputation. She couldn't deal with any more bruised egos; Maxine was at her wit's end of what other activities to engage him in. It seemed as if she had tried every hobby imaginable, but none had proved to be a good fit for the boy. Unless she counted Cooper as a hobby.

"Who's in the kitchen tonight, Kayla, your mom or your dad?" Kylie asked. "I need to know who's making the garlic knots so I can order them the right way. Mrs. Patrelli never uses enough butter. She's always trying to cut me back. She probably thinks she's doing me a favor because she's noticed how much these hips are spreading." Kylie grabbed hold of black spandex-covered curves as if they were hunks of pepperoni.

"Kylie, you know very well your hips are the same size they've always been." Maxine countered.

Mia chimed in, always the sweet one. "You have perfect hips."

"Yeah, perfect for birthing ten or so babies," Kylie muttered, as she looked at Kayla, waiting for an answer.

"Dad's in the kitchen tonight, Miss Chatterson. But Mom doesn't think you have big hips. She just doesn't use as much butter because she's trying to save money. She told my dad that the butter she orders every week must walk out of the restaurant on its own. She also told my dad to stop staring at your butt because she used to have a butt as nice as yours before he knocked her up with six of us kids."

Maxine squeezed her eyes tightly shut. Too much information. Some adults really shouldn't speak out loud in front of their kids. Of course, she rationalized, when you had six kids, as the Patrellis did, there probably wasn't a place in the house where you could talk without a child overhearing you.

"Well, whoever is working back there tonight, let them know we want extra butter. Tell your mom that I just finished her tax return and, as her CPA, I know she can afford to spare some. And tell your dad that, as *his* CPA, he should give that pretty mother of yours a smack on *her* butt every now and again."

As Kayla laughed her way back to the kitchen, Maxine playfully shoved her friend. "Seriously, Kylie. She's only ten years old. She's the same age as Hunter."

"You don't think that girl knows what a butt is? Even sweet little Hunter knows that."

Maxine covered her ears, wishing her friend could take the comment back. She wasn't ready to start thinking of her son's preadolescent knowledge of body parts.

"It's true, Max." Mia spoke up. "Kids today are so much more advanced. I have several nine-year-olds in my hip-hop class, and they not only know what a butt is, they know how to shake it. I've had to have talks with their parents about toning it down. Who wants to see a nine-year-old gyrating like a stripper?"

Brittany, a ski instructor in the winter who worked shifts waitressing during the off-season, came to take their order and saved Maxine from thinking about kids her son's age shaking their little-girl booties in front of him. It was times like these when she dreaded being a single mother of a growing boy.

The big oak door opened just then, and all three of them turned when Hunter walked in with Cessy.

And Cooper.

Oh, come on. She thought they were going to the Snow Creek Lodge for dinner. Even on her nights out with the girls, Maxine still had to run into the man.

She slightly lifted her hand in a small finger wave toward the trio, who were assessing their table options. Oh please, let there be an empty table on the opposite side of the restaurant! She loved her son, but she did *not* want to sit anywhere near Cessy and that marine.

"Look, Gram, there's a booth right by them." Hunter practically skipped over to their table, not noticing that the adults he'd come in with weren't following. "Hey, Mom. Hi, Aunt Mia and Aunt Kylie." He greeted all of them with a quick hug, then turned back to look for his companions.

Cessy had taken off in the other direction as soon as she'd breezed inside, leaving Cooper to stand at the hostess desk and debate which one of his hosts he should follow. Maxine almost felt sorry for the poor man who started their way. It was clear he'd rather hang out with a ten-year-old boy and a gaggle of sweaty women than go rub elbows with all the local bigwigs Cessy was chatting up.

He was wearing a pair of faded jeans and some hiking boots that looked relatively new. She wondered if he'd been shopping since he'd been in town. However, his plain green polo shirt was a bit frayed around the collar, so she figured he hadn't. Of course, when she'd picked him up at the airport, he'd only had that one bag so she doubted he was pulling from a large repertoire of clothing options.

She'd yet to see him in anything besides cotton shirts and jeans.

Oh. And his boxer shorts that night.

She closed her eyes, trying to block out the sexy memory.

"Good evening, ladies," Cooper said when he reached their table. Kylie and Mia both smiled at him.

When he turned to Maxine and their gazes met, her heart flipped over, her cheeks warmed and her brain began to tingle.

"Good evening, Kayla." Hunter immediately mimicked his older friend's sophisticated line to his classmate, who was still standing at their table after delivering the bread.

The girl giggled and blushed, making Hunter stand a little straighter.

Maxine flashed back to their earlier conversation about school-age girls and she wanted to snatch her precious baby out of the restaurant, cover his eyes and forbid him to talk to the opposite sex ever again.

But she saw self-assurance in Hunter's eye and a little swagger in the way he angled his body next to Kayla. After years of worry over his lack of friends and social status, she had to wonder if his growing confidence was a good thing. And if the man standing beside Hunter was the reason for it.

Before she could think of something to say, Brittany brought their drink order.

Maxine took the glass straight from the waitress's hand before she could set it on the table. As soon as the red wine touched her lips, Cooper raised his eyebrow as if questioning her need for liquid courage each time he was around.

Sweet mercy, but the answer was yes. Yes, she definitely needed it.

She took a second sip and then a third in a show of rebellion to the assumed judgment she was probably imagining. When he raised that eyebrow even farther, she knew her assessment had been right.

"Careful, Cooper, or that brow is going to leave your forehead altogether." Maxine couldn't believe she'd said that out loud. Nor could she blame the wine, since it had barely entered her mouth and couldn't possibly have hit her bloodstream yet.

Her friends, who had been sitting there like a pair of smiling bumps on a log, finally jumped into the conversation, asking the man generic questions about his stay and what he thought of the town.

Maxine didn't know if they were saving the poor man from her rudeness or saving her from herself. Either way, she was grateful that Mia and Kylie were distracting him, even if his eyes returned to her every fifteen seconds.

Kayla mentioned something about a new pinball machine, and Hunter disappeared into the restaurant's game room with their miniature hostess. Oh, to be young and carefree again. Maxine was tempted to follow the kids to the loud arcade area in search of a more relaxing environment.

"Actually," Cooper said to Maxine before she could fully focus on the conversation, "I was hoping to talk to you about something. Ladies, do you mind if I steal your friend away for a second?"

"She's all yours," Mia said.

"You can have her for as long as you need her," Kylie added, and Maxine couldn't help the frown she sent their way.

"Do you mind if we step outside?" he asked.

She wanted to point out that it was nice he was finally asking *her* permission for a change, but she bit back the remark.

Brittany set the steaming, buttery garlic knots on the

table just as Maxine stood up. Not only did she have to talk to the sexy man alone, but now she was going to miss out on the carbs she'd worked so hard for in Pilates class.

"You better save some of those for me," she said to the two traitors, before following Cooper toward the door. She heard her friends snicker behind her back and, when she turned to make a knock-it-off face at them, she failed to see Cooper come to an abrupt halt to allow a pizza-carrying waitress to pass.

She slammed right into his hard-muscled back and placed her hands on his waist to steady herself. He covered her hands with his, looping their fingers together and drawing her outside, in an intimate conga line for two. Her nipples tightened against his back and she tried to tell herself it was the cold mountain air and not the way he kept her tightly wrapped against his body.

They reached the empty sidewalk, and he took his time releasing her fingers before he finally turned around to face her. But when he did, she almost had to reach out and steady herself again. Those penetrating eyes were going to be the death of her.

Chapter Seven

When Maxine slid out of the booth to follow him outside, Cooper felt the familiar tightening of his jeans that happened almost every time she was around. They should make pants like hers illegal. They were black and fit her sexy legs like a second skin. He had to walk out of the restaurant in front of her because he didn't think he could keep his eyes straight ahead if she had been beside him.

Yet, when she slammed into him and touched his waist, he lost all control anyway. Well, *almost* all control. He hadn't turned around and thrown her on top of the nearest table so he could press himself against her body and kiss her senseless—which was what he wanted to do the second he saw her. But he'd gripped her hands and held her to him, refusing to let go until they got outside. He hadn't even cared who'd seen them.

He tried to look her in the eye, but his gaze kept dipping down to her athletic tank top and the taut nipples that he'd felt against his back and still stood erect. He shoved his hands in his pockets to keep from reaching his thumb out and drawing circles around the stiff peaks.

"You wanted to talk to me?" she asked.

He hated to be reminded of what they were doing outside in the first place, although he'd sure enjoyed the way they'd gotten out here.

"Yes." He cleared his throat, barely trusting himself to speak. "I got an email from a guy I know with the Florida Department of Corrections."

Her face went blank, but it could have been the wine or lust dulling her expression. Man, he hoped it was lust.

"You know. Florida? Where that Nick guy is in prison?"

"Oh, yes! Of course. Wait, why would you get an email about Nick?"

"Because you seemed concerned about your friend. So I looked into it for you and contacted my buddy who works out there. Anyway, I wanted to give you the heads-up because I figure you would know the best way to talk to Mia about it."

"You did that for Mia?"

He sighed. "Contrary to your opinion, I'm not a self-centered jerk who is above doing a favor for someone. I just…don't like to see anyone living in a state of constant fear. And I *really* don't like guys who hurt women." What he left out was that he'd also done the favor for Maxine in an attempt to get in her good graces and to somehow prove himself to her.

Luckily, she was too curious to ask any more about his reasons.

"So what happened?" she asked.

"Basically, they conducted a shakedown of his cell." At her confused expression, he explained. "A shakedown is like a random search where the guards look for contraband and stuff. Anyway, they found a big stash of pictures, probably taken from a telephoto lens, of Mia and the outside of the Snowflake Dance Academy. The photos were inside a manila envelope with a Boise postmark dated last month. Since Galveston has a no-contact order with his victim, they were able to formally write him up for rule infractions. That means the parole board will find out that he's been collecting current info on Mia and will most likely deny him."

"Oh, my gosh!" She put one hand on his bicep and one to her mouth, as if holding in her disbelief. "That's awesome. I can't believe you did that. Thank you, so much. We need to tell Mia. She's going to be so relieved."

"Listen, I know it sounds like good news, but the fact remains that this creep has had someone spying on your friend and relaying information to him. The parole delay is just a temporary fix. Mia is still going to need to be on the lookout for whoever Nick hired to tail her."

Maxine's hand dropped from his arm, retracting the temporary warmth they'd created together. She wrapped her oatmeal-colored cardigan sweater tighter around her torso as if to ward off the evening chill.

"What do you think I should say?" she asked.

"That's the thing. You know your friend better than I do, which is why I wanted you to be the one to decide what, if anything, to tell her. You should also have her talk to the county sheriff so they can be on the lookout for any suspicious activity."

"I really don't think that's going to do much good. Damn, I wish we had better local law enforcement. What do you think we should do?" Her big blue eyes looked up at him, this time with hope instead of resentment.

She was finally coming to him for advice. Oh, how the tide had turned.

Hunter stuck his head out the door, interrupting them. "Mom, your food is here."

Great timing. Just as they were starting to feel more relaxed around each other.

"Hey, Coop, Gram is looking for you. She wants me to bring you over to meet some of her friends." Hunter looked first at his mother, then at him. "What are you guys doing out here?"

Maxine backed away from Cooper as if he were holding a grenade minus the pin.

"Nothing." She answered too quickly, but Hunter didn't seem to notice.

"We can talk about it later," Cooper said to just her, opening the door for them as they reentered the warmth of the Italian restaurant. It was interesting that when they talked about things that had nothing to do with the way their bodies heated every time they got within ten feet of each other, they could be perfectly civil.

"Coooooooper," Cessy Walker called out before the big oak door closed behind him. "Come over here. I have some people I want you to meet."

"Oh, listen." Maxine turned back and leaned toward him, placing her mouth as close to his ear as she could without drawing more attention. "I forgot to warn you about Hunter's grandmother. She can be a bit overwhelming most of the time, but she means well."

"So I've gathered."

"I'll just apologize in advance for anything that comes out of her mouth."

It wasn't the apology he'd hoped for, but Maxine Walker was definitely softening toward him. And when he was this close, the intoxicating scent of vanilla lingering on her skin made him anything but soft.

"If you were really sorry," he said, "you'd come over there with me and run some interference."

"Not on my night off." She smiled, not looking the least bit remorseful. "I deal with her and her cronies all the time. You're on your own, soldier. Good luck." She smiled as she patted his arm, then headed back to her friends.

Yes, that had definitely been a smile. And another touch—which the two waiting women had obviously seen because they were giving Maxine questioning glances as she made her way to their table. Those ladies obviously hadn't learned the meaning of the word *subtle*.

"Cooper?" Cessy called again, waving him over like an airport traffic controller guiding a 747.

He straightened his shoulders and strode over to a large table where she stood by several local businessmen.

What could they possibly want with him?

Maxine had finished an entire plate of baked ziti and three cold garlic knots by the time Cessy had made her way to the table, with Cooper trailing behind her.

"Girls," her mother-in-law said by way of greeting.

Kylie offered her a sunny smile. "Hi, Mrs. Davenport."

"Kylie Chatterson, you know good and well that I took back my family name after my last divorce."

"Of course, Mrs. Davenport-Walker. Or is it Mrs. Walker-Davenport?"

"Stop your teasing, Kylie." Cessy forced her Botox-treated face into a smile. "Why can't you call me by my first name like you do the others? After all, I'm just one of you girls."

Maxine felt guilty for not being more welcoming, so she scooted over and patted the booth. "We already finished eating, but you can join us if you'd like to." Was she ready to include Cooper in that invitation?

"No, dear, but thank you. I just wanted to stop by and let you know that I introduced our pen pal to Mayor Johnston and some of the city council members over there." Cessy looped her arm through Cooper's as if she'd gone out to Afghanistan herself to purposely find him and bring him back to Sugar Falls. "We're trying to convince Cooper here to throw in his hat for the new chief of police position they just approved."

Maxine almost felt sorry for the poor marine, who looked as if he'd rather be in a prisoner of war camp than in an Italian restaurant with the best small-town networker who ever lived. Unfortunately, he probably hadn't realized he was already in the tight clutches of Cessy Walker's master scheme.

Obviously, Cessy had given him her rare stamp of approval, which was more than a little surprising. Maxine had thought she'd make a big deal out of Hunter's relationship with him. But, apparently, the man's rapport with her grandson had the opposite effect. And that meant, if Cessy had her way, they'd be stuck with Gunny Heartthrob indefinitely.

"That's right," Mia agreed. "You were a police officer in the military. It would be great to finally have some local law enforcement who could respond to calls in less than thirty minutes."

Maxine had yet to tell Mia about the news regarding Nick's parole. She'd wanted to talk to Cooper more before saying anything. But now she was worried about the idea that the former marine might decide to stay.

"That would be perfect!" Kylie chimed in. "You're looking for a police officer job anyway, right?"

"Actually, I don't know what I'm looking for. I don't even have my official discharge paperwork yet."

"But you're here to find yourself, right?" Mia asked. "You don't have any ties anywhere else, do you?"

Cessy stood there smugly, as if her foot soldiers were doing all the work for her.

"The only plan I have right now is to go rescue Hunter from the game area, and then order a large meatball sub with extra cheese. And a beer."

His smile took the edge off his quick departure, and Maxine had to hand it to the guy. He sure knew how to put a group of overly curious females in their place. Unfortunately, by the way her body was humming at his take-charge attitude, she doubted her curiosity about the sexy man could ever be sated.

Early the following morning, Maxine checked on a large vat of cream in the industrial-sized stainless steel churner. The sun hadn't come up yet, and she was downstairs, creating the handmade dough that her assistants would later transform into the fastest-selling product in Sugar Falls. This was her favorite time of day, when she was alone with her thoughts, her son still snuggled in his bed right upstairs and the promise of a new day just an hour away.

She'd just switched on the Motown station on her satellite radio and had begun to pull out the sacks of sugar and flour when she heard a knock at the back door. Her employees never arrived before seven, and they usually didn't get deliveries until the afternoon, so she felt a little uneasy. She couldn't help thinking about what Cooper had told her last night. Some creep had been snooping around town to seek out Mia.

As she made her way to the door, hoping it was someone she knew, her stomach twisted and the hairs on her arms stood up straight.

She looked out the peephole and almost ducked when she spotted Cooper's chiseled face on the other side. She had to remind herself that he couldn't see her through the wood. However, the light was clearly on and he could probably hear Marvin Gaye asking about what was going on. She couldn't very well ignore him.

Her hand shot to the top of her head, to the messy ponytail that never fully contained the strands of her wild hair. Then she chastised herself for even caring how she looked. At least her apron was clean.

She unbolted the door and cracked it open, not sure if she wanted to welcome him into her sanctuary—at least, not before seven o'clock in the morning.

Now here he was, coming to her private domain at oh-dark-thirty as if it was the normal part of his day.

When she swung open the door, he simply said, "Hey. Hunter said you're usually up early working downstairs, and since I had an idea about the Mia situation I wanted to run by you, this seemed like the perfect time."

The steam coming from his breath drew her attention to his full mouth and reminded her that, even though it was spring, it could still be bone chillingly cold up here on the mountain.

It also reminded her of the last time they stood in a doorway looking at each other. *Sweet mercy.* She opened the door wider and stepped aside. "Sure, come on in."

He was wearing track pants, old sneakers and a faded camo-green sweatshirt that read Pain Is Weakness Leaving The Body.

Well, ooh-rah to that.

"I have a fresh pot of coffee," she offered.

"Thank you, I'd love some."

She couldn't believe it. They were actually being cordial to each other. And while his proximity this early in the morning was causing her insides to roil like the vat of cream in the electric butter churner in the corner, she didn't want to ruin the mood.

As she poured them each a mug, she tried to keep her hands steady, which wasn't an easy task since she felt his assessing gaze on her back.

She handed him a cup, and their fingers brushed, causing a tingle to zip along her arm.

"So this is where the magic happens?" he asked.

Did he think they were about to make some magic of their own in the warmth of the secluded kitchen?

"I've been meaning to come in and check this place out," he added, as he looked around. "I loved the cookies Hunter sent me and, according to everyone who eats at the Cowgirl Up, this is one of the busiest spots on the weekends."

"Oh. *That* kind of magic." Of course he meant the cookies. "I don't know if there's anything that special about it, but yep, this is where I make it happen." She tried to be modest about her business, but it was hard to downplay her success. Especially when they were standing smack-dab in the middle of it.

"There's obviously something special about it, otherwise, it wouldn't have been featured on *Good Morning, Boise!*"

"Oh, you heard about that?"

"Did I mention that I've had breakfast at the café every morning since I arrived? I think I'm caught up on all the happenings within a hundred-mile radius of Sugar Falls. Anyway, what's the secret to producing the best cookie in Idaho?" He slid his free hand into the front pouch pocket on his sweatshirt and took another sip of coffee.

"Not really any secret. Want me to show you around?"

"I was waiting for you to ask if I wanted a tour." He

rolled back onto the heels of his feet, as if unable to keep still, and smiled over his mug.

Oh, sweet mercy. There was that dimple she'd seen in the picture he'd sent Hunter. It softened his face and made him look less tough.

Put yourself in check, Max. It doesn't matter that he's sexy as can be, he's not for you.

She turned toward the storefront and motioned for him to follow her.

She led him to the public part of the shop, which had a trendy decor that was both cute and homey. She'd gone for the shabby-chic cottage look with white woodwork and yellow gingham accents to match the trademark ribbons used to tie the boxes of cookies. Wicker baskets lined the shelves, and held prepackaged cookies wrapped in cellophane for the customers who didn't want to wait in line. And there was almost always a line on the weekends, thanks to the big spread that had showcased her shop in a premiere travel magazine listing the Sugar Falls Cookie Company as one of the top twenty must-visit places in Idaho.

"So what else do you make here?" he asked, as he walked around, sizing the place up as if he were a prospective buyer.

"Just cookies. I thought about trying cupcakes and muffins, but I really wanted to focus on one product and perfect it. We usually carry fifteen different varieties, plus the pick of the month. But the beauty of my operation is that all of my cookies are based off the same basic dough. That's what I was doing when you came in—making the starter dough. Then we add the necessary ingredients to each individual batch to customize the flavors."

"Holy crap!"

She turned back at his shocked outburst and saw him

holding a package of cookies at arm's length, as if trying to assess it from a distance.

"Twenty dollars for a dozen cookies?" he blinked his eyes several time, as if not believing what he was seeing. "Duncan's Market has Chips Ahoy! on sale this week for two ninety-nine."

She grabbed the package and put it back in its display basket. "These are slightly better than Chips Ahoy!, you know."

"Oh, I know, all right. Hunter sent me some in the hospital, remember?"

No, she didn't remember. In fact, Hunter had probably done it without her knowledge. But she'd give his indirect compliment its due. "Thank you."

"I just had no idea how much they were worth. No wonder you can afford such a nice car and apartment."

"It also allows me to afford the top quality ingredients that go into each batch. Besides, it took a lot of hard work and tight budgeting to get where I am."

"I don't doubt that. So why cookies?"

She'd been ready to do verbal battle because that's what she'd come to expect from Cooper. But he stood there at ease, looking at her with genuine interest. And ever since their talk last night, it seemed as though they'd arrived at some sort of common ground. And what could be more neutral than cookies?

"You don't really want to hear this, do you?"

"Why wouldn't I?"

"Okay, but let me get you another cup of coffee."

He followed her back to the kitchen and, after she refilled his mug, he leaned against the long butcher block counter, a captive audience.

Well, her dough wasn't going to make itself and since it gave her an excuse to avoid his assertive gaze, she took a deep breath, then began to measure the ingredients she knew by heart as she talked.

"When Bo died, I was almost twenty-four years old. I was a new widow with a twenty-month-old little boy to support, and completely disillusioned."

"Did you have any family? Besides the fabulously worldly and socially connected Cessy Walker?"

When she rolled her eyes, he smiled, and she realized he hadn't succumbed to her mother-in-law's posturing and showboating last night.

"My family is pretty much spread all over the world. My parents are career army and I was tired of moving and determined to put down roots. As far as my mother-in-law being supportive, Cessy had adored Bo and thought he could do no wrong. We'd always had a decent relationship, and she was crazy about Hunter—still is. But she was too lost in her own grief and had a complete breakdown when Bo died. Not that I could blame her. I can't even imagine how I would react if I lost…" She couldn't even finish the thought. "Anyway, Cessy took off with the first rich man she met a few weeks after the funeral, which we now refer to as 'The Unfortunate Husband Number Four Incident.'"

He chuckled. "I could see Cessy doing that. Hunter says she's been married quite a bit. What about you? You didn't want to get remarried?"

"No way. I really didn't want to get married the first time, but I wanted to give my child a family life and se-cure home. In my mind, that meant marrying his father. But commitment and fatherhood weren't exactly what Bo had imagined."

"What *had* he imagined?"

Maxine was ready for the freshly churned butter and went to retrieve the large bowl. Cooper helped her lift the stainless steel vat up onto the counter and peered inside. "Wait, before you answer that, what's this white stuff?"

"It's butter."

"It doesn't look like butter." He grabbed a metal spoon from beside the coffeepot on the counter, dipped it into the bowl before putting a dollop of the stuff into his mouth.

She thought of the way that frothy cream was probably melting in his mouth right this second, and she wanted to melt right along with it.

Focus, Maxine.

"I…uh…get the cream delivered here fresh from a nearby organic dairy. Then I churn the butter myself. It's my secret ingredient and it's what gives my cookies that decadent texture."

He tossed the spoon in the sink, grabbed a clean one, then dipped it into the bowl and took another taste. She could sit here all day and watch him do that, but the dusky rays peering through the front shop window reminded her that the rest of the world would be waking up soon.

"So, Bo…" he started, leading her back on track.

She sighed. "Bo was what some people would call a big fish in a little pond."

"How so?"

"Well, he grew up here in Sugar Falls, star football player and the apple of his overindulging mother's eye. He'd been handed everything his entire life and told that he was the best and should expect big things. He even had me convinced he was greater than life—for a short time, at least. But in college, he couldn't live up to the perceived hype. He never even started in a game, and there certainly wasn't any interest from the NFL, as he'd expected."

"That must have been a blow to his ego."

"It was. He would tell his mom and his friends back home that the coaches had it in for him or that the next game would be his big breakthrough. But honestly, he really wasn't all that great. I mean, he wasn't horrible—he'd made the team as a walk-on player, but I was on the football field every Saturday and had a good understanding about the game, and he didn't have what it took to start for a top-ranked university.

"When we were still at college, he knew he didn't have to play the big man about campus with me. But the minute he moved back to Sugar Falls, with a pregnant wife in tow, he started putting on the show again. He was back to his small pond, and he no longer needed me to keep him from getting lost in the big sea that was college. He started drinking a lot and spending more time with people who didn't know he wasn't the big deal he thought he was."

"Did he cheat on you?"

Maxine was so absorbed in mixing her dough that she didn't mind the personal nature of the question. Of course, she was in the safe haven of her kitchen, and it was hard not to be herself in here. "Probably." She shrugged. "But by that point, I honestly didn't care enough to know one way or the other. I'd had Hunter, and he was the true love of my life. In fact, we barely saw Bo unless Cessy forced him to clean up his act and think about his family. His mother likes to remember only what she wants. I get so frustrated when she tries to sell her son as some standout pillar of the community, especially since *she* was the one who always had to find him new places to work whenever his bosses would get sick of him not showing up or for drinking on the clock. In fact, she'd just used her last connection to get him a job at a used car dealership outside of Boise when he drove one of the cars off the lot after a three-martini lunch. He crashed into a guardrail, dying instantly. And now Cessy is rewriting history. But I guess if I were her, it would be easier to focus on what could have been. All of us mothers like to think the best about our kids."

Maxine finished the first batch of dough and started another. She no longer had to work on the weekends, but Fridays were their biggest baking days and she needed to get everything prepped for her staff.

"So Bo got a big head and couldn't deal with not being who he thought he should be on or off the football field?"

"In a nutshell."

"Is that why you have a problem with Hunter playing sports?"

"Yes. No. I don't know. Maybe one of them." She looked up from her prep area, afraid of the disapproval she'd see in his eyes. Instead he gave her a look of understanding.

"I can see where that comes from." Cooper settled in more comfortably against the counter. "In the sporting world, it's a thin line between friendly competition and inflated egos."

"Exactly!" For once, someone finally got it.

"So you were left alone and needed to find a way to earn some income." He steered her back to the cookie business, and she wondered how he'd gotten her to reveal so much. He must be a good cop.

"Yes. I was down to my last twenty dollars and was going to a mommy-and-me play group at the community center. I was supposed to bring a dessert and didn't have much in the fridge—just a couple of eggs and some heavy whipping cream that I'd accidently grabbed instead of milk when I'd been at the store with a crying toddler who had the flu and had kept me up all night. I didn't want to waste the cream or spend any more money, and I remembered seeing a documentary about the history of butter. So I looked online to learn how to churn the cream. I made the cookies and everyone went crazy for them. A couple of moms asked me to make them for different parties and they paid me. Within a few months, I was hauling dozens of them—and a wild toddler—down to the farmers market in Boise.

"A year later, Kylie had just gotten her CPA license and helped me start a business model. I was approved for a loan, probably with the help of some of Cessy's contacts down at the bank, and rented out half of this space. The upstairs apartment was perfect because it allowed me to work down here while Hunter napped. A couple of years ago, I bought the building and remodeled it and the apartment. When we got busier, I hired more help. And now I'm finally able to sit back and let loose on the reins. Although…" She shoved the second bowl to the side and started on the third. "I still like to make the dough every morning by myself. It's kind of a private ritual that reminds me of how far I've come."

"For what it's worth, I think you're doing a remarkable job with your company and with Hunter. He really is a neat kid, Maxine."

And since they were finally to a point where they could exchange kind words, she let her appreciation flow. "Thank you for saying that. And thank you for helping Mia. I know that's why you came over this morning, and here I am droning on and on about my life story."

"Actually, I liked hearing it, even if I think it's just the tip of the iceberg. And like I told you last night, I hate seeing anyone victimized. So this is how I think we should handle Mia's situation…"

There he went. Back to his man-in-charge position even though he acted as if he wanted her opinion. She lifted a skeptical eyebrow, ready to shoot down his idea as soon as it was out of his mouth. But she bit her tongue while she waited for him to continue.

"Since you obviously know Mia better, I think you should tell her that I've made a few calls and it looks like the whole parole thing isn't going to go through. You know, kind of ease her mind. Then, after the hearing, hopefully my buddy will have more information for me about how Nick got the pictures. Once she gets the official word that his parole was denied, I'll talk to her about what they found and give her some tips and pointers for being on the lookout for suspicious people, although she seems to think everyone is suspicious."

Boy, he sure hit the nail on the head with that observation.

"In the meantime, I'll start poking around and see if I can figure out who's been hanging around town and spying on her."

That seemed like a pretty solid plan and she was glad she'd kept quiet long enough to hear him out. "I know you don't want my thanks, but it means a lot to me that you're helping out with this, Cooper."

"It's giving me something to do while I figure out what I'm going to be when I grow up." He smiled, revealing those amazing dimples again. "Besides, I do have an ulterior motive."

Was this the part where he told her that he was interested in Mia? He'd denied it before, but Maxine wasn't sure where she stood with him, and not knowing put her in a jealous mindset.

"Which is…?"

"Hunter and I have been playing a bit of catch after school, and he's not too bad. Little League already did their tryouts, but one of the teams is a guy short. So they'll let Hunter play if you'll agree and sign off on the paperwork."

The wooden spoon she'd been using to mix the batter

clattered out of her hand and onto the floor. But instead of looking down at the mess, she lifted her head in surprise. She certainly hadn't been expecting *that* to be his motive.

"But you agreed with me about the sports," she said. "About the thin line and the egos and all of that."

"I didn't agree." He held up his hand. "I just said that I understood where you were coming from. But Max, Hunter loves baseball. And he really wants to play and fit in with the other kids."

Ugh. He had her there because as much as she hated it, her poor son had slowly become an outcast.

"Plus, he's a kid," Cooper added, driving his point home. "You still have control over how he sees the world and how he acts both on and off the field. Why not teach him the responsible way to play and let him enjoy it?"

She braced her hands on the counter and met his pleading stare, locking steady gazes for several beats.

"Can I think about it?" She knew she was stalling, but her heart and her mind were telling her two different things.

"The league needs the forms by this afternoon so he can be on the roster for tomorrow's opening game."

"Where are the forms?"

"Out in the Jeep. I'll go get them."

He was being more than presumptuous, but when he hurried out the door, any objections she wanted to voice died on her lips as she watched him from behind.

Gunny Heartthrob certainly had a nice butt in the track pants that were designed to move fluidly over an athlete's muscles. He was back in less than a minute and handed her the paperwork.

"Let me look them over," she said, feeling herself cave in. "If, and that's a big if, I decide to sign them, who do I give them to today?"

"Take them over to Alex Russell at the sporting goods store. He's the league chairperson. And he can hook Hunter up with the team uniform and some cleats. I already got him a glove."

"I know Alex. He's pretty big on following the rules and cutoff dates." She couldn't look at the marine without thinking of his backside in those pants so she stared down, trying to read the fine print that set the registration deadline for two weeks ago. "How'd you get him to agree to let Hunter play?"

"Did I mention they were down a player?"

"Yes, but couldn't they pull an extra kid off another team to even things out?"

"Did I mention they were down an assistant coach?"

Her eyes shot up from the paper. "You volunteered?"

"Volunteered. Was coerced. Depends on who you ask. But it's not like I have a full schedule."

"So you're sticking around for a while?" She bit her lip, calculating that the youth baseball season lasted until almost summer. That was still three months away.

"I don't have anywhere else to go. My physical therapy at Shadowview will take several more weeks."

"What about the police chief job here in town?" She held her breath, not sure what she wanted his answer to be.

"I don't know. I don't want to make any permanent decisions yet. I'm not used to small towns, and I haven't evaluated all of my options. I need to concentrate on getting my knee better first."

Before she could respond, Hunter's voice sounded from upstairs. "Yeah, Gram, Mom's right here." Her son was still in his pajamas, the cordless phone in his hand when he reached the bottom step. "No, you're not bothering us. She's just in the kitchen with Cooper. Hey, Coop, are you staying for breakfast?"

Oh, no. Maxine lunged for the phone, but the implication was already there. No telling what Cessy thought.

Still, that didn't solve her bigger dilemma. Cooper may not have spent the night, but he was certainly staying for the next few months.

Chapter Eight

The pain in Cooper's knee pulsed all the way up his thigh and hip and was spreading into his back as the physical therapist at the Shadowview Naval Hospital maneuvered his leg. He'd rather deal with the pain, though, than have his thoughts cloud over, dulled from the drugs. He still didn't remember what he'd said to Maxine when he'd last taken his prescription, but he wasn't going to risk it again. It had taken a while, but they were finally in a good place.

Hell, after the way he'd heard Cessy whoop it up on the other end of the phone receiver this morning, the whole town was going to assume that he and Maxine were in much more than a good place. And he wasn't sure how he felt about that, although he'd hightailed it out of the cookie shop so that he wouldn't have to hear her denials.

"Are you taking any pain medications?" The shorter Asian man, who'd told Cooper to call him Jeffrey and looked as if he could bench-press a compact car, asked as he pushed Cooper's knee almost into his chest.

"No," Cooper grunted out, not willing to swipe at the sweat dripping off his forehead.

"Not even a little something to take the edge off, Gunny? It doesn't make you less of a man or a marine. You just had two major surgeries rebuilding pretty much your entire leg. I promise you, when our session is done, you're going to *want* something to ease the agony."

"Great. I'll be looking forward to it." His voice sounded labored even to his own ears, but he wasn't being sarcastic. He really was looking forward to getting off his butt and running again. And if having this guy twist him up into a pretzel would speed things along, then bring on the pain.

Being in the therapy wing brought back the memory of his recent hospital stay. The first surgeon at the naval base he'd been airlifted to said he was lucky the blast from the bomb hadn't taken out his whole leg. Instead, he'd just shattered his kneecap, severely damaging his tendons and meniscus, when he landed on it following the impact that had knocked him off his feet. But he didn't feel so lucky. They may have been able to replace his knee with an artificial one, but no military doctors could replace everything he lost. Not his dog. Not his squadron. Not his Corps.

Not his life.

Well, not his life as he'd once known it. Plenty of soldiers had lost a lot more than their stupid kneecaps, so his injury was nothing in the scheme of things.

Cooper squeezed his eyes shut as he moved to a stationary bike, trying to tell himself the pain was of the physical variety and had nothing to do with the feelings he'd forbidden himself to think about.

But listening to Maxine open up this morning had caused some sort of sympathetic crack in his own dam and, for the first time, he needed to take inventory of his emotions.

Man, he hated dealing with any pain, physical or otherwise. He reverted to his standard operating procedure and switched gears from thinking with his heart to thinking with his mind. And his mind was telling him that he needed a job and a game plan. Maybe he was no longer fit for the military, but he could still be a cop somewhere. Sure, the government would most likely give him some medical benefits and a little disability money, but then what?

If he was honest with himself, this Sugar Falls chief of police position would actually be a pretty good gig for him. He was more than qualified and Lord knew the town needed someone like him with honesty and integrity to lead them on this new venture. He'd been researching the idea and found out he'd have to do some training at a supplemental academy to learn the ins and outs of Idaho state law. But to have a department of his very own? To have a hand in selecting his own employees and forming the entire force from the ground up? That was a cop's dream.

Sure, the little town wasn't what he was used to and it was a far cry from the poor, overcrowded neighborhood where he'd grown up. But he'd never fit in there, either.

After Cooper finished ten minutes of pedaling on the bike, Jeffrey flipped the emotional switch back on when he said, "So I was reading your file before you came in. Man, it must be a hard thing for a man to lose his career and his dog all at the same time."

"Yeah, well he wasn't really my dog." Maybe if Cooper denied it out loud, he could deny it in his heart and it would help ease the pain.

"Uh-huh." Jeffrey motioned for him to follow to one of the blue cushioned tables. "From what I read, that dog followed you all around the base. Ran PT with you, ate with you, slept with you. Everything a man's best friend should do."

Cooper still said nothing. He had no idea what a best friend should do. He'd purposely avoided making friends. Sure, there were men he liked, men he trusted, men he'd depended on. But that was where his personal connections ended.

"The report said your dog saved your life." The therapist continued, not taking Cooper's silence as a hint that he didn't want to talk about it. "That suicide bomber was headed straight for you when your dog attacked him and detonated the bomb."

He'd done his best to forget that fateful run and all that had followed.

He'd been airlifted to the nearest military hospital. They'd stabilized him before transport to Okinawa, but his knee was shot. And as the memories resurfaced yet again, Cooper could still smell the singe of flesh in the air.

"Yeah, well, they don't call it a war zone for nothing." Cooper didn't know what to say. Before his hospital release, the counselors from the PTSD unit came by to see him, but he'd refused their services and their patronizing handouts.

"So what's your plan?" The body-builder-turned-wannabe-shrink wrapped his knee in hot towels. "Is Idaho home for you now?"

That was the thing. Cooper didn't know where home was. Yet. But he was starting to get an idea of where he wanted it to be.

"I'm staying with some…uh…friends up in Sugar Falls." Well, one friend, singular, but after this morning, when Maxine had finally let down her guard, Cooper was hoping to make it plural. Hell, who was he kidding? He wanted to be way more than just friends with the sexy cookie queen.

"Ah, man, I love that town. We try and do a kayaking trip up there every year, and my girlfriend is crazy for this bakery up there. Have you been to the Sugar Falls Cookie Company?"

Great. Even in a military hospital, still panting from the pain of a tough workout, he couldn't get away from the woman. And, as he smiled through his final stretches, he didn't know if he wanted to.

"You *do* know you're wearing a minidress and high heels to a Little League game, right?" Maxine watched Kylie expertly navigate the aluminum bleacher stand while Mia followed close behind.

"Listen," Kylie said as she plopped down on the seat in front of Maxine and Cessy. "I'm a redhead with the skin complexion that goes along with it. I don't look good in yellow, so it's not a main staple of my wardrobe. This was the closest thing I had to the team colors on such short notice."

While dropping off Hunter's baseball paperwork yesterday, Maxine had picked up a yellow T-shirt for herself when Alex Russell told her that parents usually showed support for the kids by wearing the team colors. Too bad her son hadn't been assigned to the Avalanches. She would've been set with her almost-all-white attire.

"Besides," Kylie continued, as she made room for Mia to sit beside her, "I have to judge a pageant tonight and need to leave straight from here. What's wrong with my outfit anyway? It's Dior." She tugged at the hem of her tight black dress with thick yellow piping—either in an attempt to maintain some sort of modesty or to just keep her rear end from direct contact with the cold metal seat.

"Well, in that case, it makes perfect sense that you'd wear couture to the ballpark on a Saturday morning." Mia, who was usually the quiet voice of reason, was known to launch a zinger when they least expected it. Kind of like a sniper of sarcasm.

Maxine scanned the bleachers, checking out the other spectators. She wasn't used to feeling out of place in most situations, but she didn't like the attention their black-and-yellow-clad foursome was attracting from the parents of the opposing team. She sat up straighter, reminding herself that they were there to support Hunter.

"Some of the fans over there look pretty intense," Mia observed.

At least Maxine wasn't imagining things. She'd been right. Organized sports were too competitive and Hunter was going to get his heart broken if he didn't play as well as people might expect of Bo Walker's son.

Cessy made her well-practiced, socialite finger wave toward the bleachers on the other side of home plate—a born networker. "They're probably jealous that the four of us are the best-looking cheerleaders this town has ever seen."

Kylie's hair whipped back as she shot an incredulous look at Cessy. But Maxine shook her head, silently warning her friend not to hurt the older woman's feelings. If she wanted to think she was one of them, then let her.

As the players ran out on the field, Cessy shot out of her seat. "Let's go, Bumblebees!"

"They're the Yellow Jackets," Maxine corrected.

"Same thing."

"Who's the Hottie McHotterson in the dugout?" Kylie asked, pointing to a man wearing a team jersey and kneeling down in front of Hunter.

"That's Cooper," Mia stage-whispered.

"Right. The sunglasses threw me off. They make him look all elusive and official. So, he's taken up coaching now, too?" Kylie turned around with a grin that would've made the Cheshire cat jealous. "Gunny Heartthrob is becoming quite embedded in your family life, huh, Max?"

"Speaking of embedded..." Cessy leaned in like the co-conspirator she longed to be. "When I called over to their house *very* early the other morning, Cooper was there for 'breakfast.'" Her mother-in-law used her diamond ring-adorned fingers to simulate air quotes over the last part.

When Mia and Kylie looked at Cessy with big eyes, the older woman nodded and grinned. "Mmm-hmm."

"He was *not* there for breakfast," Maxine defended. "And he most certainly was not in my bed or embedded in any other way."

The smiles and nods continued.

"Stop smirking at me," Maxine said to Mia and Kylie. Then she turned to Cessy. "And you shouldn't encourage them." Before she could continue her scolding, which wasn't turning out to be very effective anyway, she spotted her son. "Oh, look, here comes Hunter."

The boy was the last player to come out of the dugout, making his way slowly behind the batter's box and looking like a sausage encased in padded gear.

"Why is he playing catcher?" Maxine stiffened. "Is that the loser position? Are they making him play that because no one else wants to wear all that crazy big gear?" As she anxiously moved to the edge of the seat, her knees bumped Mia's back.

"Settle down, Max." Mia pushed her legs back and gave her a reassuring pat. "Don't be one of those over-the-top parents we talked about the other night."

"Actually," Kylie said, "the catcher position is one of the most important roles on a baseball team. Remember, my dad was a pitcher? He said a catcher is always in tune with not only his team, but with the other batters, as well. And he calls the pitches."

Her friends' words were only slightly comforting. She shaded her eyes and looked toward Cooper, who ran out to Hunter and showed him where to stand.

Oh, no! What if her son got too close to the batter and ended up taking a baseball bat to the head? Was that helmet strong enough to withstand a hit like that?

Cooper must have sensed her worry because, as he jogged back to the dugout, he caught Maxine's gaze and gave her a thumbs-up.

"Good catch, Hunter," Cessy yelled, causing Maxine to pivot her head to see what she missed.

Kylie sighed. "Mrs. Walker, the pitcher is just warming up. There's going to be a lot of throws coming Hunter's way. You can't yell into our ears every time he catches one."

Bless her friends. Maxine wouldn't have been able to take the added stress of Cessy's constant cheering if she didn't have them to help rein the woman in.

Hunter's movements were slow and awkward the first couple innings—probably because he had to wear all that uncomfortable gear. When their team was at bat, he sat mostly by himself in the dugout, with only Cooper talking to him.

Did the other kids think he wasn't any good? Were they ostracizing him? She wanted to run around the chain-link fence and tell him to get in the car so she could drive him home.

But by the third inning, he seemed to be getting the hang of things. He even caught a pop-up foul ball, forcing an out. When he turned to look at her and smiled that big freckle-faced grin, she finally allowed her clenched body to relax.

The first time Hunter went up to bat, Cooper fitted the helmet over his curly head, and then knelt down to talk to him. Hunter nodded and walked up to the plate. Cessy jumped up so fast and was so excited that Mia had to tell her to stop shaking the entire bleacher stand.

After two strikes, her son finally hit the ball and made it to first base.

"He hits far enough," a dad sitting a few feet away from them said to another man. "Maybe if he ran faster, he would've gotten to second base."

"Hey," Kylie called out to the guy.

Maxine cringed at the defensive insult she expected her friend to throw his way, but Mia grabbed Kylie's arm.

"This is his first time playing," the sweet dance instructor told the opinionated dad. "He's still getting the hang of things. Plus, we're all on the same team, right?"

The man smiled at Mia, and the woman next to him elbowed him in the ribs.

Bless her friends again.

By the eighth inning, Hunter was moving around in the catcher's gear as if it was his second skin. Maxine had to admit that he really wasn't half-bad. Cooper had been right. And she hadn't been able to stop looking for her son's mentor every time Hunter made a good play. So far, they'd shared at least four smiles and two thumbs-up, not that she was keeping count.

"Okay, girls," Kylie said. "I have to take off if I'm going to get to the Miss Royal Cupcake pageant in time." The sexy redhead gave them each—even Cessy—a hug, and then navigated her stilettos down the bleachers.

The dad who'd smiled at them earlier got another elbow in his ribs when he tilted his head to watch her walk toward the dugout, and Maxine had to cover her mouth to keep from chuckling out loud.

Kylie said something to Hunter, who grinned and nodded before waving goodbye to his quasi aunt. Then she said something to Cooper and pointed back at Maxine. He lifted his sunglasses, looked her way and then burst out in full laughter.

Were they making fun of her? Maxine suddenly wished Kylie was still sitting in front of her so she could slink down and hide. Or so that she could kick the woman in her barely covered rear end.

She hadn't decided which would be the better option.

When Kylie teetered off toward the parking lot, hips swaying in pageant-perfected confidence, Cooper shot Maxine another thumbs-up. But this time, she had a feeling that the approving gesture had nothing to do with Hunter.

What in the world had her friend said?

And why had Cooper found it so amusing?

Over the past few weeks, Cooper had seen Hunter just about every day. He'd also caught glimpses of the boy's mom, but he hadn't really had an opportunity to get her alone as Kylie had suggested at the opening game.

He'd tried to think of reasons to show up at the bakery in the early-morning hours, but since Mia had gotten word that Nick Galveston was being denied parole, and Cooper hadn't had any success at finding out who he'd paid to spy on Mia, he didn't have anything to talk to Maxine about—besides Hunter. And it was tough to talk to her about the boy because she prickled up any time he made a suggestion that was out of her Mama Bear norm.

But that Friday, when he was on his front porch restacking firewood, he looked out to the main road and realized he finally had his chance.

Through the trees, he spotted a pair of bright orange

running shoes and tanned legs quickly making their way north of town. He looked down at his watch. It was a little after nine. From what he'd been able to gather, Maxine's regular morning routine consisted of making her dough in the bakery before Hunter woke up, then having breakfast with the boy before taking him to school. After she dropped him off, Hunter said she usually went for a long run before opening up the trendy cookie shop at ten o'clock.

But Cooper hadn't realized her jogging route went right by his cabin. He shook his head as he stacked the last log. Man, he couldn't believe that he was already starting to think of the place as his. Or that his cop skills were getting rusty not being put into use daily. He needed to get back to police work. And in order to do that, he needed to get back into prime form.

He quickly calculated that if she had to be in town no later than ten, she would probably be turning around pretty soon and heading back this way. Good thing he'd worked extra hard at physical therapy yesterday and that Dr. McCormick at the naval hospital finally gave him the green light to start running again.

He went inside and threw on his shorts before lacing up a pair of old sneakers. He hadn't replaced the ones he'd been wearing in the blast and, after seeing them in the clear plastic belongings bag a nurse gave him after his surgery, he threw them straight into the trash. He knew he couldn't look at them without thinking of Helix or the explosion that had ended his military career.

Cooper did some lunges and stretching exercises, then made his way through the trees toward the main road. He couldn't very well lie in wait for her to get close before popping out of the woods at the exact moment she ran by. That'd be way too obvious.

Since he'd have to start out slow, he figured that Maxine would easily catch up to him, making a chance meeting more plausible. Man, was he seriously resorting to plotting and scheming just to spend time with the woman?

He started at an easy pace, heading south. His knee was feeling okay, but he knew that if he ran all the way to town, it would be two miles. He could probably make it there without too much soreness, but he didn't think he could do the roundtrip. At least, not on day one.

He'd been running for about fifteen minutes before the strains of The Commodores met his ears, and he turned back to look for the music's source. Maxine was keeping a pretty good momentum and had her phone strapped to her arm, acting as a mini stereo. He kept his legs moving, trying not to be too apparent as he turned his head to watch her approach. She slowed down when she got to him, and he cursed himself for not being able to maintain her quicker pace.

She was wearing a sports tank, and had her long-sleeved shirt tied around her waist. She probably wasn't ready to start cooling down, but she slowed her speed to match his. "You get the okay to take up running again?"

"Yep, first day out."

"How's your knee feeling?"

Like hell, he wanted to groan. "Like I could go another ten miles," he said instead.

"Yeah, that strained grimace all over your face looks like you're ready to enter the Idaho Potato Marathon."

"I'm not making this face because I'm in pain. I'm making it because you have that crappy music turned up so loud." The station had switched songs to a slower tempo.

"Crappy music? How can you say that about Smokey Robinson? Aren't you from the Motor City?" She began picking up speed—probably on purpose because he'd insulted her.

Why did he always set her off? Gregson would have told him it was a coping mechanism to keep her from hurting him first. But for some reason, he seemed to be hurting himself. *Literally.* His knee was on fire, but he forced himself to meet her unspoken challenge.

"I'm from the part of Detroit that's more about Eminem and Kid Rock. Now, *that's* music you can run to. This stuff makes me want to meet up with Johnny and Susie by the punch bowl so we can sock hop to some doo-wop in the high school gym."

"Whatever. This music gets inside your bloodstream, makes you want to move."

He looked at her breasts, tightly constrained in her sports bra. Oh, man, how he suddenly envied Smokey. Cooper wanted to be the one who got in her bloodstream and made her move.

He was so busy looking at her bouncing form that he missed seeing a small pothole. Just as he stepped in it, a sharp pain bolted through his knee, and he pulled up, knowing he'd jarred something.

"If the music is that bad, I can put on my headphones. I normally don't like to wear them when I'm on the mountain road so I can hear cars approach." She glanced back at him. "Hey, are you okay?"

She put her hand on his arm, her eyes full of concern. The sympathy in her expression almost took the edge off the pain. Almost.

They stood there on the side of the road, less than half a mile from town, both breathing hard, but he refused to sit down and rest. He'd gone almost two miles and had no idea how he'd limp back to the cabin. Damn his pride for pushing him too hard on his first day out.

"Stretch it out a little." She knelt down and rubbed her hands over his scar. The throbbing wasn't as bad now that he'd stopped running. He looked down at the curly blond hair piled on top of her head, his fingers itching to feel it.

If she didn't stand up and he wasn't careful, he'd have to deal with a different kind of throbbing. And, if that happened, her face would be right at eye level—or mouth level—

"It's fine. Really." He backed up and limped around before he could let his thoughts run away with him. "I just need to walk it off a little."

"Cooper," she called. When she caught up with him, her gaze snagged his, and her expression as well as her tone grew serious. "I don't think you should put any more pressure on it until the swelling goes down. Don't walk all the way back to your cabin. You're going to do more damage."

"Well, I can't very well sit out here on the side of the road until it feels better." Although, that was exactly what he wanted to do.

"We're almost to town. Let's go back to my shop. Then I can drive you home." She had her arm around his waist and was already steering him south on Snowflake Boulevard before he could refuse.

He wanted to be tough, to pretend that nothing was wrong and that he could take care of himself. But he also wanted to spend more time with her. And he didn't mind the way she felt, nestled up against him like that.

As they headed toward town, he didn't say anything or put up much resistance. He hobbled slowly, but the pain was already lessening. It was almost ten o'clock by the time they reached the back entrance to the bakery, where several cars belonging to her employees had already parked.

"Aren't you guys opening soon?" he asked.

"Is it ten already?" She looked at the clock on her phone, and he felt like a tool for taking up so much of her time this morning.

"Listen, you don't need to take me home," he said. "I'll go over to the Cowgirl Up and get something to eat. Then I'll try to get a ride home with someone."

Three months ago, if anyone would've told him that he'd be in some cutesy small town hitching rides from strangers, he would've laughed his head off. But he'd been eating regularly at Freckles's restaurant, and the townspeople weren't such strangers after all. Not that he opened up much about himself, but someone always struck up a conversation with him. And what had started out being annoying had become…well, sort of expected. And he'd gotten used to it. People in Sugar Falls were just that way. He had a suspicion a lot of their friendliness and interest in him had to do with getting Cessy's stamp of approval, but everyone treated him as if he was a born local, even if he was still waiting for the boot to drop.

"The breakfast crowd is mostly gone by now," she said. "The only ones who might still be there are Scooter and Jonesy. What are you going to do? Climb up into Klondike's saddle and trot on back home?"

He chuckled at the image.

"Besides," she continued, "you need to get that leg elevated and iced right away. Why don't you come up to the apartment and rest it. I only need to open the shop and get the staff set up for the weekend. I can give you a ride home in an hour or two."

She cracked the back door to look inside and, before he could see what was going on in the industrial-sized kitchen, she pushed him toward the stairway, practically lifting him up the first two steps.

"Are you trying to keep your employees from seeing us go to your apartment together?" He put his hand along the rail, trying to brace most of his weight so he could hobble up the rest of the way.

She flashed him a guilty look, and he waited to hear her denial. Instead, she peeked her head out of the stairwell. "Everyone should be in the front setting up the display cases. I don't think they saw you."

"Would it be horrible if they did?"

"Not horrible. I just don't want anyone getting the wrong impression. It's one thing for my girlfriends to tease me about you mercilessly, but I shouldn't have to explain my personal life to my employees."

What did he expect her to say? That she'd be honored to spend time with him? That she'd like everyone to think they had something intimate going on? He knew from experience not to get his hopes up, especially with a woman like her. She had a reputation to maintain. And Cooper wasn't the kind of guy she wanted to parade around town. So it was good that she was spelling things out. Time to go back on high alert.

"I got it from here," he said more severely than he'd intended when she'd opened the apartment door and tried to help him inside.

She startled as she stepped back, and he regretted his abrupt tone. But he needed to put a little distance between them, especially if she didn't want the two of them to become any more gossip-worthy.

And judging from the knowing smirks and prying questions at the café and the market and the Little League field, the townspeople were talking already. It wouldn't take much to prove to everyone that where there was smoke, there was fire.

"Fine. Go lie down on the sofa. I'll get you some water and some ice and then I need to shower and head back downstairs." While polite, her tone had cooled considerably.

"Sorry." He glanced down. "I didn't mean to snap at you like that. I guess I'm hurting a little more than I'd like to admit." Well, that was partly true. Except it was mostly his pride that was hurting.

"Thank you," she said as she opened the freezer and reached for an ice pack.

"For what?" He'd been a jerk, and now she was thanking him?

"For acknowledging that you're human."

He ran his hands along his running clothes, trying to decide if they were too sweaty to sit on her white couch. His shorts were fine, but his T-shirt was still fairly damp so he took it off before settling onto the down-filled cushions.

She put a water bottle on the coffee table, then froze when she turned to hand him the ice pack.

"What's wrong?" Had he messed up her perfect throw pillow placement?

She stared at his chest. "You're not wearing…uh…you took off…" Color rushed to her cheeks and her eyes shot up to his before returning back to his torso.

She was totally checking him out. And judging from both her inability to finish her question and from the tightening of her nipples under her sports bra, she liked what she saw. He wanted to pump his fist in triumph, but something about the situation gave him a weird feeling of déjà vu.

Her gaze finally returned to his face and he smiled. In response, she threw the ice pack at him and practically ran down the hall, slamming the bathroom door behind her.

Chapter Nine

To: hunterlovestherockies@hotmail.net
From: mcooper@yahoo.net
Re: Shirts
Date: April 15
Hunter, tell your Gram that I already bought a suit so she can stop worrying about my wardrobe. Also, tell her that I appreciate the shirts she bought me when you guys went to Boise yesterday, but I don't look so great in pink stripes or the "new spring patterns." Contrary to what she told you, the G.I. Joe look is always in style. I know she means well, but how do I tell her no more shopping trips on my behalf?
Cooper

Maxine checked the clock on the wall above the stainless steel bakery sink. It was almost one o'clock, and she took off her apron, intending to turn over the shop reins to her weekend manager. She needed to drive Cooper home, but when she'd gone upstairs to check on him an hour ago, he was still sleeping. So she'd made a turkey and provolone sandwich for herself to take downstairs and one for him to eat when he woke up. She'd also left a note telling him to make himself at home and propped it beside a bottle of ibuprofen in case his knee was still hurting.

She couldn't believe she'd acted like such a blushing prude who'd never seen a man's bare chest. In the shower, she'd resolved to act as if nothing out of the ordinary had happened. She didn't want to succumb to a repeat performance of that first night he was in town when she'd gone back to his cabin. Luckily, by the time she came out of her room to go downstairs, he was sound asleep on the couch. She threw a soft blanket over him before hurrying out the door.

Hopefully, he still had the blanket covering him when she got back up there. She took each stair as though she was a convicted death row inmate—dead woman walking. With each echo her boot heel made on the wood step, she reminded herself, *I am a mother. I am a businesswoman. I am mature enough to handle a half-naked man in my home.*

But when she tiptoed into the room, she saw that the sofa was empty. The white throw was neatly folded by the stacked pillows, and the plate holding the turkey sandwich wasn't where she'd left it.

Where in the world was he? Had he come downstairs and slipped out the back door while she'd been working?

The green shirt he'd been wearing earlier now lay wadded up on the floor near the coffee table. He wouldn't leave without that, would he?

She walked around the kitchen, not wanting to think of what she'd do if she found him in her bedroom. Luckily, a ribbon of light glowing from underneath the bathroom door explained where he was. Good. At least he was awake and able to move around.

The empty sandwich plate rested in the sink. She rinsed it off before putting it in the dishwasher, then fumbled around in the kitchen, trying to make herself seem busy. The bathroom door clicked and, realizing he was coming out, she quickly opened the freezer, afraid to make eye contact with him. She even kept her back turned, pretending that she was looking for something deep inside the subzero depths.

She barely heard him approach, but the fresh tang of her eucalyptus soap swirled in the air.

"I hope you don't mind, but I took a shower." His comment forced her to turn and acknowledge him, but the moment she laid eyes on his damp and masculine form, she froze.

Whoa. He was wearing his shorts, thankfully, but his hair was wet, and he was still shirtless. As he walked toward her, she couldn't take her eyes off the muscles rippling in his chest, which was dusted with hairs that trailed below his waistband.

"Maxine?"

She couldn't answer. She was too mesmerized by his ripped abdomen.

"Maxine?" he said again, and she had to drag her eyes upward as if they were heavier than ten-pound bags of flour.

He stepped closer, and she leaned back against the kitchen counter to steady her shaky legs.

"Huh?" she managed to get out.

Cooper was now only inches away. He lifted his hand to her face, his fingers skimming her cheek and setting her skin on fire. "If you don't stop looking at me like that, I'm not going to be able to control myself anymore."

She didn't want him to control himself. And she was sure as heck tired of controlling herself. So she raised her lips in invitation.

And that was all it took.

His hand slipped to the back of her neck and he pulled her in for a searing kiss. His lips were soft and warm, yet demanding. But no more so than her own. She leaned into him, opening her mouth, seeking more of him. Her fingers traveled up his bare torso, exploring the coiled tension in the muscles of his chest. He angled his head, deepening their kiss—and her response.

Besides that moment at the cabin, it had been a long time since she'd been kissed. Or since she'd wanted to kiss anyone. Could he tell?

She was a runner and knew she should be pacing herself, but the intense sensation of his stroking tongue made her want to sprint to the finish line.

She pressed her body in tighter against his, feeling the strength of his desire through his thin athletic shorts.

This man made her body melt just as quickly as he made her temper flare. Instead of fighting it, she embraced the heat, craved it. She would have asked for more, but her mouth was so busy, her only utterance was a soft moan.

He must have understood perfectly because he let go of her hair and grabbed her hips. Before she knew it, she was weightless. She felt the cool granite of the countertop through her jeans. Her legs parted to draw him in closer, then wrapped around him to keep him there.

One of his hands pressed against her lower back, pulling her against his arousal. His other hand tugged her blouse free of her waistband, then made its way upward, until his fingers reached the lace of her bra.

It was too much, yet at the same time not nearly enough. Her body buzzed, and her mind raced trying to keep up.

She arched her back, filling his palm with her breast, while he nipped at her swollen lips.

"You like this?" he asked, grazing a thumb over her nipple.

She nodded, ready to rip open the buttons of her shirt to give him more access.

"I've been dreaming of this ever since that first time I saw you," he continued, his lips trailing down her neck.

"I wanted you to hold me like this again, but I thought you hated me."

"I could never hate you."

As he started unbuttoning her blouse, she gripped the counter as leverage so she could push the throbbing center between her legs against him, knowing that only his body could ease her ache.

But he stopped and stared at her.

Had she been too forward? Did he think she was out of control? Had she done something wrong?

"Did you say hold you *again*?" he asked.

She nodded, unlocking her ankles and slowly letting her legs dangle off the countertop, not sure how things had shifted so suddenly. Or why. She sat up straighter and tried to pull the ends of her shirt together.

But his fingers still held her buttons and he wasn't letting go, even though he continued to look at her with less passion and more clarity. "When did we do this before?"

"That first night at the cabin, when I brought you the groceries. You opened the door in your..." she gestured at his running shorts, which weren't much more than boxers now "...and, well, it wasn't like *this*, but you...uh...you know. Things were... Well, we got all caught up in..."

Damn. Could she sound any more like an idiot?

"I thought I dreamed that."

At least he hadn't completely forgotten. "Nope, it wasn't a dream."

"Then, thank you." His hands slid down to her thighs and moved them back into position around his waist.

"For what?" Her mortification hadn't lessened, yet her legs pulled him in tighter, the damn traitors.

"For the groceries." He kissed her neck. "For coming back that night." He kissed her jaw. "And for this." His lips dipped back down to hers, just as her cell phone blasted out the theme song from *Indiana Jones*.

"Hunter!" She scrambled back so unexpectedly, she launched herself halfway across the counter and almost into the sink.

"Oh, crap. Where is he?" Cooper turned to the door, while trying to tug his nonexistent shirt into place.

"The phone." Maxine reached her purse. "Hunter's calling me. That's his ringtone." She took three breaths and heaved herself off the granite countertop before sliding her finger across the screen.

Cooper let out a sigh and ran his hand through his damp hair. While she answered, he limped over to the sofa and bent to retrieve his shirt.

"What's up, sweetie?"

"Who's supposed to pick me up from school today?" Hunter asked. "I'm pretty sure it's not Cooper because he's usually here a few minutes before the bell rings."

Her gaze flew to the clock on the microwave, and she grabbed her purse. How could she have gotten so caught up in lust that she'd nearly forgotten her child at school?

"I'm on my way. I got tied up in the…" When she caught a glimpse of Cooper's smug expression, she had to turn away. "Ah…in the kitchen. I'm leaving right now. Are there any teachers you can hang out with until I get there?"

"There's always someone in the office. And in the detention room."

"Just give me ten minutes." She had her keys in her hand and was walking toward the door when Cooper waved his arms in the air in the silent universal signal for, "Hey, look over here."

What? She asked with her eyes since she couldn't very well say it out loud.

"I need a ride home," he mouthed.

Damn. She couldn't very well leave him at the apartment. And she couldn't take him home first and abandon Hunter at the school any longer. How was she going to deal with this?

If sharing a heated kiss with Gunny Heartthrob had just complicated her life, how much more complicated would it become when Hunter saw the two of them arrive together, especially if Cooper didn't wipe that smug grin off his face?

"That's so cool that my mom was driving by and could give you a ride home," Hunter told Cooper as Maxine pulled out of the school parking lot. "Just think, if she hadn't been late to pick me up, she never would have seen you limping on the side of the road."

Cooper stretched out his knee, trying to rub away the tenderness. He felt guilty about misleading the boy, but not as guilty as he would've felt if he'd finished what he and Maxine had started on that kitchen counter.

It wasn't as if they'd done anything wrong. They were two healthy, single adults. Both of them would've been physically satisfied, but he had a feeling she would have regretted it afterward. Maxine was a mom with high standards and a reputation to consider, and Cooper wasn't any woman's idea of a long-term commitment.

Not to mention, Hunter was like his... Well, he didn't quite know what Hunter was to him, but it was a lot more than a pen pal. Cooper'd never gotten to experience the father–son relationship, but he imagined it might be something similar to what he and the boy had.

Did he honestly think the parental role he experienced with Hunter would easily transfer over to a corresponding bond with the kid's mom, as well?

No way. He wasn't relationship material—and he had the divorce decree to prove it.

Besides, Maxine had made it clear that morning in the bakery that she wasn't looking for a second husband. And on several occasions she'd gone overboard in conveying that she definitely didn't need a replacement dad for her son. Not to mention, every time they were in public, the woman acted as if he was an embarrassing case of foot fungus.

He could take a hint.

It didn't stop him from wishing that Maxine would get off her girl-power kick and see that Cooper could be a nice addition to their lives. Of course, he wasn't going to be the one to force the issue and risk rejection. If they went that route, she would need to come to that realization all on her own. But in spite of the way she'd looked at him earlier and her heated response to his kiss, he sensed that enlightenment might not come at all, especially since she thought her association with him might mar her stellar position in the community.

He and Maxine hadn't said a word to each other during the short drive from the bakery to the school, and he decided he'd follow her lead.

For now.

If she wanted to pretend that nothing had happened between them, then he'd go right along pretending with her.

Cooper had grown up being ignored and Lindsay, his ex-wife, had taught him the art of the silent treatment. He'd been such a great student that he'd learned to stop caring when a woman was giving him the cold shoulder.

Unfortunately, Maxine had such sexy, soft shoulders, which had been anything but cold when she nestled up under him when he'd limped back into town. And there was no way he could ignore them or those long legs that had wrapped around his waist and held him so tightly just minutes ago.

Crap.

He looked down at the swelling in his running shorts and adjusted his seat belt. Of course, Maxine chose that exact moment to look at what he was doing. He clasped his hands together in his lap and looked out the window, desperate to find something neutral to talk about.

"Does it smell like rotten chicken in here to you guys?" Cooper asked.

"It totally does. Mom said she got one from the store a few weeks ago and it leaked all over the back. She sprayed some air freshener in here, but the stinky smell is coming back."

Maxine's cheeks flushed a rosy shade of pink, and she kept her eyes glued to the road, apparently not wanting to talk about the chicken any more than she wanted to talk about what had gone on in her kitchen earlier.

"Anyway," Hunter continued, apparently not noticing the tension between the adults in the front seat, "since it's spring break, Jake Marconi is having a sleepover at his house next week, and he invited me."

Maxine kept her eyes on the road. "I didn't realize you and Jake had become friends."

Cooper had seen the boys talking together more now that they played on the same team, and there was less competition between the two. But he kept his lips shut, hoping Maxine would come around without him putting in his usual two cents.

"Jake's all right when he isn't totally full of bull," Hunter said. "Besides, he hasn't called me Chubba Bubba in a long time."

Maxine flinched at the hated nickname, but still kept her eyes straight ahead.

"Also," Hunter added, "he picked me to play the soccer goalie at recess yesterday."

"Who is going to this sleepover?" Maxine asked.

"Just some boys from my class and some of the other guys on the team. I guess Jake has one every year, but this is the first time I got invited."

"Let me call Mrs. Marconi and talk to her about it first, okay?"

"Sweet!"

Cooper didn't turn around, but he could imagine Hunter pumping his fist in the air. The kid had made big improvements in the fifth grade popularity scene, and he hoped Maxine had noticed. She was probably being cautious before sending her cub into what she might consider the social lion's den. But she was definitely making progress, too.

"You can probably talk to his mom tomorrow at the game." Hunter tapped Cooper on the shoulder. "Hey, Coop. Is your knee going to be better for the game tomorrow?"

"I wouldn't miss your game, kiddo."

Or your train of thought. He'd learned that the ten-year-old could bounce conversations around like his brain was the flipper on that new pinball machine at Patrelli's.

"What about trout fishing on Sunday?" the boy asked. "Can we still do that?"

"Hunter!" Maxine said. "Let Cooper's knee rest a little. You have all week off school to hang out with him."

Cooper didn't know why her attempts to limit their time together bugged him. She'd told him in the diner that she didn't want her son to become a pest, but he had a feeling it was more than that—in spite of what they'd just shared.

"Buddy," Cooper said, "we can hang out every day— if it's okay with your mom." If she was really concerned that Hunter might become a burden, then that ought to appease her. He actually liked hanging out with Hunter. And he didn't want Maxine to put the brakes on their relationship just because she didn't like where things were headed back there in her kitchen.

"Sweet," Hunter said again. "Every day is good for me, except for Friday. That's the night of the sleepover."

Cooper stole a glance at Maxine and saw her roll her eyes. So he'd been right. She wasn't just trying to protect Cooper's privacy.

"Hey, Coop," Hunter said. "You want me to ask Jake if you can come, too? He said his dad always has to sleep in the doghouse, but maybe we could bring our sleeping bags outside with you guys."

Maxine smirked, and Cooper mentally kicked himself.

"No thanks, Hunter. You need to spend some quality time with your school buddies. Besides…" He purposely brushed his fingers along Maxine's shoulder under the pretense of bracing his hand on her seat, then turned to talk to the boy in the back. "I *really* hate being in the doghouse."

Maxine lifted an eyebrow at him, then flashed her gaze back to the road. She was barely giving him an inch. But it was better than shutting him out.

"Hey, Coop," Hunter said, changing directions again. "I got your email, but I didn't tell Gram yet that you hate the new shirts she picked out for you. Mom says when Gram buys us something, we have to smile and say thanks, even if we don't like it."

Maxine now got her own chance to smirk.

Cooper heaved a sigh. "I liked them. Kind of. I just don't want her wasting her hard-earned money on clothes for me."

"I don't think she works that hard for her money because she sure does like to spend it. Anyway, you probably don't need a fancy suit anymore because she told Freckles that Mayor Johnston and the rest of the city council owe her a favor, so you'll probably be a shoot in for the new chief job."

Shoo in. Shoot in. Cooper had learned that it was all the same to Cessy Walker as long as she got what she wanted. Heaven help him if the society matron ran this town the way she picked out men's clothing. But he held his tongue, not wanting to complain about the woman who thought she was doing him a favor. He knew his résumé and his experience was what would ultimately land him the position— not Hunter's overbearing grandmother.

The Explorer pulled into the long, narrow drive and, even though Maxine took the bumps much slower, he rubbed the ache in his knee.

"We'll come in and get you settled, right, Mom?"

"I…uh…we…" She looked at Cooper as if to ask him to give her an out.

He shook his head at her. Nope. She'd left him to the wolves in the Italian restaurant, first with her mother-in-law and then with her nosy friends. It was time for payback. "That'd be great. Thanks, Maxine." He winced as he stretched out his leg, overdoing his invalid act. "I could really use some help getting to my bedroom."

"I'll get an ice pack." Hunter ran into the cabin ahead of them so Cooper didn't have to exaggerate his limp.

"You big faker," Maxine said, as she came around the car and walked close enough so her son wouldn't overhear her. "You had no problem lifting me up earlier, but now you can't make it inside?"

"I got it!" Hunter raced back out to the porch, a frozen blue pack in his hand.

"Oops." Cooper pretended to stumble, then threw his arm around Maxine, pulling her close while making it appear that she was the one bracing him.

Her elbow dug into his rib cage, and he suddenly felt a kinship with Jake Marconi's dad. In response, he pulled her tighter against him, restricting her movements and preventing her from doing any more damage.

"Take it easy, Mom. You're going to hurt him if you keep pulling back like that."

Cooper's chuckle turned into a very real yelp when Maxine's boot heel landed squarely on his sneaker-clad foot.

"Whoops," she said. "I guess I lost my footing carrying all your *dead*weight."

If that was a threat, he was enjoying himself too much to care. "Better put me on the couch," he said, as they barely squeezed through the front door together. "I know the countertop is probably where you'd prefer to have me, but you can tend to me just as well down here."

He was quick enough to dodge the heel of her boot this time, but he almost missed the couch with the force she'd used to shove him on it.

"Here's the ice pack, Mom." Hunter tossed it to her and Cooper was impressed when she easily snatched it out of the air. "I'm gonna go check on the fishing gear for Sunday."

The minute the boy was out of the cabin, Cooper braced himself for the tongue lashing he well deserved for playing possum.

She surprised him by walking toward his kitchen table and asking, "Is that the plant I gave you when you were in the hospital?"

"Yeah, it's really perked up."

"It's huge! If it perks up any more, you're going to need to get it out of that pot and transplant it into the yard."

"Oh, I don't know. I've never really been the type to put down roots anywhere—literally or figuratively." Except now that he'd spent some time with Maxine and Hunter and the comfortable town of Sugar Falls, he second-guessed whether he was still intent on not settling down.

"That's too bad. I don't think things can reach their potential unless they're truly grounded."

Were they still talking about the plant?

"I don't know about that. Some things get so embedded in one spot that when there's an upheaval in their whole ecosystem, they wither and die instead of getting successfully uprooted and moving along to the next garden."

"So you're saying you'd rather go through life in a cheap flower pot from the drugstore?" She lifted that sexy blond eyebrow at him.

"I'm just saying that I haven't found the right pot to contain me. So until then, I think I'll just keep on rolling."

"You mean like a tumbleweed?" She snorted. "You know, no matter how big and prickly a tumbleweed gets, all it takes is one little car to hit it and, whack—nothing but thorns blasted to smithereens."

"Can I get you a beer?" He stood and barely limped to the fridge, away from her and the emotions she was bringing out of him. Now that Hunter was outside, he didn't need to play the injured role. He pulled out two bottles of pale ale from a brewery that had just opened down the street.

"That'd be great."

He grabbed a bottle opener out of the drawer and popped the top for her. "Glass?" he asked.

She thanked him when he handed her the icy mug, then took three breaths before downing a big gulp.

He liked to rile her up, but he hadn't meant to be such a jerk she'd needed to cope with alcohol and deep breathing exercises.

"Hey, I'm sorry about earlier. I was just trying to tease you and lighten the mood."

"It's not just that." She sighed, then took her glass to the denim-upholstered sofa and sat down. He liked the way she was making herself at home—and he definitely liked the way she looked on his couch. "I can't believe I forgot my own child at school. What kind of mom does that?"

He took a seat next to her, wanting to rub her back or touch her in some way to ease her stress. But she was sunk so deeply against the pillows, there was no way to touch her—unless he touched the front of her body. And look at where that had gotten both of them before.

"It's not that big of a deal," he said, placing his foot on the coffee table, elevating his knee. "Nobody ever picked me up from school and Sugar Falls isn't exactly the toughest neighborhood. Besides, Hunter didn't seem to be bothered too much by it."

"And now this sleepover thing? What if the other kids tease him? He's never stayed overnight at a friend's house."

"He's spent the night with his grandmother before, right?"

"But this is different."

"It's a little different, but at least you know that he can be away from home for the night. Plus, I don't want to toot my own horn or tell you I was right all along, but playing baseball has been really good for his confidence. He's getting exercise and he's fitting in more with the other boys his age. Not to mention, he's one hell of a catcher."

"I don't know if I'm ready for him to grow up."

She hadn't had another sip of her beer since that initial swallow, but she still held the cold glass in her hands, turning it this way and that.

"Max." Cooper took her mug and set it on the coffee table. "*He's* ready. And he's going to grow up whether you're prepared or not. Besides, if you're afraid to stay alone, you can always come have dinner out here with me."

Sure, the last part was a cheesy line, but he hoped that if he made the offer sound like a joke, he could better play it off when she turned him down flat.

Instead of slapping him and walking out the door, she looked at him with such an intensity he wondered if he'd made the suggestion in one of the Afghani dialects.

"Do you think anyone would find out if I did?"

If she did what? Was she actually considering going on a date with him? And if so, why would she want to keep it on the down low? But if it meant getting her alone one evening on his domain, he'd keep whatever secret she wanted.

"I wouldn't tell anyone." He wasn't completely sure that they were talking about the same thing until she turned toward him and put her hand on his bare leg.

"You promise? Not Hunter, not Cessy, not the girls?"

Oh, man. She was serious. They were definitely on the same page.

"It took me a long time to build up not only my business, but my reputation, which can be very challenging for a single mom. I don't want anyone in town talking about us."

"Maxine, I think people have already been talking. Personally, I don't mind people thinking that someone like you would want to date someone like me. I get where you're coming from as far as the reputation thing goes, but you're human and you're allowed to be attracted to a single man. I sure as hell am attracted to you, and if we decided to take things to the next level, then we'll keep that decision to ourselves."

"That's what it'd be, right?" She looked at him. "No ties. No promises. Just dinner?"

Hell, it wasn't as if he was thinking in terms of forever, but he wouldn't mind being more to her than a one-time thing.

Yet before he could say so, Hunter ran back in the cabin.

"All the gear looks pretty good, but we'll need to get some fresh bait. Hey, Mom, did you know that your shirt is buttoned up all wrong?"

Chapter Ten

On Sunday evening, as Hunter and Cooper set a red plastic cooler down on her expensive hardwood floor, Maxine placed her hands on her hips. "I can't believe you brought those smelly fish into our house."

Did they think she was operating a seafood restaurant?

"C'mon, Mom. Me and Cooper cleaned them and everything already. You're the best cook I know, and I promised him that if he took me fishing, we'd eat what we caught. Besides, if we don't have the trout tonight, then we have to go to Gram's for that same ole chicken she always gives us."

"Actually," Cooper said, as he knelt by the cooler and opened the lid, "I don't think it's the fish that smells so much as your son's clothes. He and Jake got into a fish fight at the cleaning station and were throwing trout heads and guts at each other."

Maxine leaned in and sniffed Hunter's Colorado Rockies T-shirt. "Oh, Hunter, that's disgusting. No wonder you stink to high heaven." She pointed to the hall. "Go take a bath right now. We're going to need to burn those clothes."

"Dang it," Hunter said as he moped down the hall. "If I knew we were gonna be burning clothes, then I would've worn those purple skinny jeans Gram got me."

Cooper laughed, and Maxine couldn't help smiling with him.

After Friday and the kitchen-counter incident, she and Cooper had fallen into a mutual understanding that they weren't going to talk about either the kiss or their upcoming dinner when Hunter went to his sleepover. But she could tell by the way he'd looked at her yesterday at the ballpark and then this morning when he'd picked Hunter up, he was thinking about next weekend just as much as she was.

Since she'd met him, they hadn't even shared a meal—not counting that awkward breakfast at the Cowgirl Up the day after he arrived in town. Maxine thought that maybe their date would seem more relaxed and less formal if they ate together first.

But she also didn't want to push him into some awkward family dinner situation that would make him feel caged in. She hadn't been with another man since Bo, and she didn't want to come across as lonely or desperate, or worse, inexperienced.

Maybe if she kept things between them informal and casual, then she wouldn't have to worry about getting hurt when he left town. And if she kept things quiet, she wouldn't have to worry about being known as the woman who had two different men ditch her.

"So how many fish will I be cooking all of us for dinner?" she asked, as Cooper pulled out the contents of the cooler. She hoped her question sounded like an invitation, but not one that he would feel obligated to accept. She didn't want to make him stay if he didn't want to.

"We just have two." He set the newspaper-covered bundles on the counter. "But if you don't think it's enough, I used to be stationed in Beaufort and learned how to make some pretty good hush puppies. Do you have any cornmeal?"

He turned to the sink to wash his hands and she wanted to do a cheer jump in excitement. He was staying for dinner. It was almost like a quasi pre-date—except with a ten-year-old chaperone.

She went into the pantry and pulled out the items they'd need to fry up their impromptu Southern-style meal. She wished she'd brought home that batch of sweet potato cookies they'd been experimenting with for the flavor of the month, but she'd figure out dessert later. If it were just the two of them, she knew exactly what she'd want for dessert. And, oh, my, how delicious he looked.

His worn jeans fit as if they were made for him, and his black T-shirt still bore the hint of fabric softener— and not the eau de fish Hunter had trailed in. Maybe he'd changed before he brought her son home. The thought that he wanted to look—and smell—good for her, made her want to follow her mental high jump with a back handspring.

"Where do you keep your mixing bowls?" he asked as he threw a dish towel over his shoulder.

Sweet mercy. She liked a man who was comfortable in a kitchen.

"Bowls are up in that cupboard." She pointed to the right side of the sink. "And pans are underneath the counter. Make yourself at home."

He looked at her midriff, which had been exposed when she was showing him where everything was kept, and she clenched her stomach muscles at the reminder of what happened the last time she'd told him to make himself at home.

She struggled with the urge to ignore the heated moment or act upon it, pondering her next move while removing milk and eggs from the refrigerator. Then she turned on the small stereo on the counter, filling the kitchen with vintage rhythm and blues.

On second thought, she moved back to the fridge for the chilled bottle of white wine she'd been saving for a special occasion.

She also had a couple of bottles of beer left over from her brother's visit last summer. Did beer expire?

"I was going to have some chardonnay." She held up the bottle. "But I have Heineken if you'd prefer something a bit more manly."

"I'm plenty comfortable with my masculinity." He pulled two goblets off the shelf above him. "Besides, I always like to have wine whenever I listen to Marvin Gaye."

At the mention of the singer who was filling the room with lyrics about getting it on, her cheeks warmed. Damn. She hadn't meant to go *that* far in setting the mood.

While balancing the wine and salad items she'd just pulled from the fridge in one arm, she lunged for the dial, spinning it until it landed on the next available station. "I promise that just so happened to be on the radio. I'm not trying to seduce… I mean, I didn't put that on to make you…"

"Hey." He reached out and stroked her shoulder, sending a shiver of heat through her core. "I know you're not trying to set the mood or stage some grand seduction, especially with your son in the house. It's just an impromptu fish fry and a couple of mature adults cooking in the kitchen."

She nodded, even though she was cooking, all right. And she had the heated body parts to prove it. Maybe she should put out some chips and salsa. Of course, if she did that, she'd probably scarf down the whole bowl in an attempt to calm her nerves.

The bathroom door clicked open and Hunter's footsteps padded to his room, reminding her that there wasn't anything inappropriate going on. At least, not tonight.

"Besides." Cooper lowered his voice as he reached to take the bottle from her tense fingers. "You already had me seduced a long time ago, and it didn't take any music or wine on your part."

Her pulse sped out of control and her arms turned into noodles. Thankfully, he reached for the corkscrew and didn't see her nearly lose her grip on the spinach and cucumber.

Was he saying that she'd unwittingly seduced him? As if he'd been hanging around town for the past weeks, thinking about her the exact way she'd been thinking about him?

She needed to sit on one of the kitchen stools and catch her breath—or at least regain use of her weak limbs. But she didn't dare let him know how unbalanced she was. So she shook off the effects of his gaze, of his words, of her pulsing hormones.

She'd no more than placed the rest of the needed ingredients on the counter when Hunter came out of his room wearing his Boise State pajama pants, which were way too short.

When had he outgrown them?

"I found that Hobbit movie I was telling you about, Coop. We can watch it after dinner. Hey, why are you guys listening to polka music?"

Maxine blushed again when she recognized the strains

of an accordion coming out of the small speaker under the kitchen cabinet. Cooper must think she was a complete basket case, acting like an awkward adolescent with her first schoolgirl crush.

Hunter turned on the television and Maxine glanced back at the man in her kitchen. His hands kept slipping on the bottle, and he was obviously struggling to get the cork out. It was a relief to see that he was equally affected by their growing attraction. She was also relieved that he was proving to be inexperienced in the art of wooing women with a fine California chardonnay.

The two of them really needed to get it together. Geez, even a couple of fifth graders like Hunter and Kayla Patrelli could maintain some sense of suave sophistication around each other. Maybe they needed a pinball machine in here to break the ice.

Cooper finally opened the wine and poured them each a glass, then they settled into a silent partnership in the kitchen. She battered the fish and got it started in a pan, while he stood beside her at the stove, dropping cornmeal batter into hot oil. As they utilized the side-by-side burners, they continued to bump into each other—although she wasn't sure it was always done inadvertently.

A bead of perspiration trickled between her shoulder blades. If her arm grazed against his one more time, she'd be jumping out of the frying pan and straight into the fire.

"If you'll keep an eye on the trout," she said, unable to take the heat in the kitchen, "I'll start working on a salad."

"What am I watching for?" He looked her up and down, and she had a feeling he wasn't talking about the fish.

She took a drink of wine and opened the fridge again before answering him. "When the edges start turning brown, just flip it."

She took an inordinately long amount of time looking

for more fresh produce that she kept well organized in the crisper drawer. But the open refrigerator provided a cold breeze, and she needed all the cooling off she could get.

How in the world was she going to control herself until date night Friday?

She finished chopping the salad just as the handsome man in her kitchen pulled the fish and hush puppies off the stove and arranged them on a white serving platter.

"Hey, Hunter," Cooper called into the open living room as he started mixing what looked to be homemade tartar sauce. "You want to get the table ready for dinner?"

Suddenly, the moment felt a little too real—as if they were an actual family having a normal Sunday dinner. Her hands trembled as she whisked the homemade salad dressing.

She couldn't afford to let him get so entwined in their lives, and she'd sworn to keep him at a distance. But, considering how close he and Hunter were, it was already too late. He'd been in town almost a month and already people were beginning to talk a lot about Cooper applying for the chief of police job. A part of her liked the idea of having him around permanently, but she suspected he was just doing it to appease Hunter and Cessy.

Last Monday, when Maxine had met Mia at the diner, Freckles mentioned how much the locals liked the former marine and how they were starting to think of him as one of their own. She could almost imagine him settling into Sugar Falls despite the fact that he was a city boy and the town's total population was less than the number of pieces in her son's Death Star Lego set.

But then she'd overheard Mayor Cliff Johnston telling the Kiwanis members that Cooper was way overqualified to be a police officer in a place like Sugar Falls and that they had better consider some of the other applicants.

Maxine always knew that Cooper's time here would only be short-term. And when things had gotten physical between them two days ago, she convinced herself that dating the man wouldn't be a big deal since he was only passing through. A relationship between them didn't have to be anything serious. But she wouldn't overthink things tonight. Instead she'd enjoy his company and the meal.

Hunter kept the conversation going through dinner, telling stories of the fishing trip, and then launching into a series of "remember whens" about his and Cooper's adventures these past weeks. When had Cooper become such an integral part of her son's memory bank?

The guys laughed all through dinner and while they did the dishes afterward. Maxine smiled at the appropriate times, but as they all piled onto the sofa for the after-dinner movie, she couldn't concentrate on wizards, or golden rings or any of the inhabitants of Middle Earth.

All she could think about was how things between her and Cooper had blown way past the serious line and straight into the "Danger: Do Not Enter" zone.

So then why was she blatantly throwing caution to the wind and charging full steam ahead?

Cooper had been running with Maxine every morning this week. Since Hunter was out of school for spring break, she wasn't going as far as she normally did, and he hadn't felt right about trying to keep her away any longer than necessary by sidetracking her or otherwise waylaying her back to his cabin. So he'd struggled and panted and matched her strides a little more every day, biding his time until tonight—when Hunter had his sleepover, and hopefully, Cooper had his.

Date, he reminded himself. It was just a date. But if a sleepover happened, so be it.

Several more hours.

Already his mood had lightened, and the fact that he was now up to three miles was an added bonus.

"It's not a sprint," Maxine said, as they neared his driveway. "You need to pace yourself."

"Yeah, you've said that about eight times this morning, Coach." Cooper's response lacked its usual gruffness, probably because he was too winded to bluster.

"And I'll probably keep saying it until you stop being such a macho he-man who won't listen to what's best for him."

She was a bossy little thing. And she was fast. But he didn't mind because running next to her while she wore her sexy skintight running gear was all the incentive he needed to get his knee back to where it needed to be.

"Stretch," she commanded, as she jogged in place, preparing to leave him at their designated meeting spot before she continued down the mountain and back to her regular life.

She'd been friendly and helpful when it came to exercising and training, but the closer it got to tonight, the more she seemed to avoid making eye contact with him. Was she getting shy or having second thoughts about having dinner alone with him? She didn't really seem like the nervous type once she made up her mind about something. But then again, maybe she hadn't made up her mind.

Neither one of them had brought up their date tonight, but Cooper didn't think he could stay away from her much longer. He was also tired of the emotional distance she maintained between them whenever Hunter was around—or when they were in town at the same time.

He put his right leg back, lunging to stretch out his muscles, and considered the best way to confirm their plans without sounding like an anxious teenager on prom night.

Man, what was wrong with him? He was a trained investigator who suddenly couldn't even ask a woman a simple question.

But what was he supposed to say? He finally blurted, "I bought a suit and I'm supposed to be able to pick it up this weekend. I was thinking we could go to Boise for dinner tonight if you didn't want to come here."

She stopped jogging in place and wrapped her arms around her bare midriff, looking right and left at any cars that might be making their way up the mountain road. Was she worried someone would overhear them way out here in the boonies?

"Sorry," he said. "I meant for that question to come out a lot smoother than it did."

"I know. I wasn't sure if we were still…uh… That is, if you wanted me…" She glanced up and down the road again, and he smiled, relieved that she seemed just as nervous as he was.

"I definitely still want you…for, uh, dinner. To eat dinner. With me."

She lifted her face to his. He was about to give her a preview of his plans for tonight when a delivery truck chugged past them, followed by a cavalcade of weekender cars presumably making their way to the Snow Creek Lodge, which had converted from ski season to whitewater rafting season.

She backed away quickly and began her jogging in place thing again, the epitome of discretion. "I don't drop Hunter off until six, so that might be a little late to head down the mountain. We can just stay here if you want. Should I bring anything?"

"Just yourself." He smiled as a motor home loaded down with bikes and a canoe lumbered by. "So I'll see you after six?

She nodded, then took off running back down the mountain as though she didn't want to talk about it anymore.

She might be skittish about what would unfold tonight, but at least he didn't have to worry that she wouldn't show.

Now all he had to do was figure out what to do with himself until she did.

Cooper had just lit the fire and turned the burner off on the stove when he heard a knock.

This is it.

He wiped his palms on his jeans and took one last look around the cabin, wondering if he'd gone overboard in setting the mood—lighting a fire, setting the table for two....

He opened the door and, although he'd been preparing all day for Maxine to show up, he still had to catch his breath when he saw her standing on his porch. She was wearing those low-waist jeans he loved and a new white top that barely reached the top of the denim.

"Hi," she said, shifting from one booted foot to the other.

"Come in." He waved her inside, then kicked himself for neglecting to put on any music or to light the candles he'd found in one of the drawers. "I was about to open some wine."

He gestured to the kitchen, but faltered when she was slow to follow. Did he sound like he was making a romantic sales pitch? He might as well have worn a shirt that read, "Please be so impressed with my hosting skills that you'll sleep with me."

"Dinner smells great," she said, placing her purse on a chair.

"Thanks. I've never really done much cooking since I've always lived on base and ate most of my meals at the chow hall. I was going to just pick something up, but I didn't want to place an order for two while I was in town and get the gossip mill rolling."

"Thank you for that."

He could be as discreet as any cop, but he was a proud man and wanted to believe that she thought he was good enough for her and wouldn't be embarrassed for people to know they were dating. If that wasn't the case, then she shouldn't be here in the first place.

While he hated the thought of her calling his bluff and leaving, especially for that reason, he shook off the negativity and squared his shoulders. "Anyway, I went to Duncan's Market to pick up something for dinner. I was going to get a roasted chicken, but they said they only sell those on Sunday." When she wrinkled her nose, he hoped it wasn't because she hated poultry. "So I had to figure out something easy to make."

"You did this yourself?" She lifted her eyebrow and headed to the stove.

"I tried. I'm not making any promises."

She picked up one of the pan lids. "What is it? Chicken and artichokes?"

"Yes, with a side of orzo. I was looking for a one-pan type of recipe that someone with my limited culinary skills couldn't mess up too badly."

"It looks delicious." She smiled as she replaced the lid. "And I'm flattered that you went to so much trouble. We might domesticate you yet, soldier."

Lord, he hoped so, because he was starting to enjoy being in the kitchen with this woman, although he knew better than to get too comfortable.

But damn, that was hard to do.

"Don't give me too much credit. Besides the hush puppies at your house, I can't remember the last time I cooked for a woman."

That wasn't the truth. He remembered exactly when he'd last cooked for a woman. And that was never.

"Well, I've never had a man cook for me. So it won't take much to impress me."

"Do most of your dates wine and dine you, then?" he said as he poured her a glass of chardonnay.

"Honestly, I haven't really dated since Bo died." She took the glass and looked back toward the table. "Do you have any chips or anything?"

"No, I'm still a novice at entertaining. I didn't even think about appetizers. Are you starving?"

"No, just nervous. Sometimes snacking helps calm me down."

"Why would you be nervous?" What a stupid question, given that his own anxiety level was about to make the shift from code orange to code red.

"I haven't been on a date since college. This is all so crazy. I've never done anything like this before. I don't even know how we go about everything. Ugh, I suck at this."

He couldn't help the smile that lifted the corners of his mouth. He was glad she sucked at this. In an effort to switch topics, he said, "I like your hair."

And he did. Her blond curls were loose around her shoulders, which made her seem more relaxed—as if she wasn't trying to keep her wild side locked up by some tight rubber band on top of her head. "That makes one of us." She ran her fingers through the strands, as if trying to tame their liveliness. It was, he realized, a nervous habit, and he reached out to stop her.

"Leave it. Please." He lifted her hand to his mouth, kissing first her fingertips, then her palm.

All the while, he studied her eyes, watched her gaze darken before she lowered her lashes.

He drew her arm up to his shoulder, pulling her in close before placing her hand on the back of his own neck. Her other arm followed suit, and at the same time, her lips parted, providing all the encouragement he needed.

He captured her mouth with his, and heat immediately consumed him. The desire had been building between both of them for so long that last Friday in her kitchen was only a crack in the dam they'd been trying to hold back.

But now, neither one seemed to care that the walls and barriers they'd built to keep their feelings locked up were fighting a losing battle. She pressed up against his body, and he grabbed on to her backside to hold her right where he wanted her. She was so responsive and eager he didn't think she could wait any longer than he could.

Not wanting to be a bad host—or to let her think he'd lost all control—he broke the kiss long enough to ask, "Are you hungry?"

Her only response was to shake her head before pulling his mouth back down to hers, the floodgates busted wide open.

He picked her up, and she wrapped her legs around his waist. But this time, instead of setting her on the kitchen counter, he walked her straight back to his bedroom. After all, a good host would give her just what she was craving.

He stopped near the bedside table and slowly released her, letting her slide down the length of his body. He'd thought about asking her permission to take her to the bedroom, but it wasn't as if he'd brought her in here kicking and screaming. More like clinging and moaning. She was a grown woman and seemed to know exactly what she wanted.

And judging by the way she peeled his T-shirt over his head, she *wanted* him, even if her fingers trembled after she dropped the soft cotton on the floor.

As her hands coursed along his chest and shoulders, every muscle in his body tensed in anticipation of her exploration. He kissed her again before returning the favor and helping her take off her own top.

Her breasts were beautiful, sitting up firm and high in her white lace bra. He'd imagined seeing and tasting them since they'd first met. In fact, he wanted to see and taste every bit of her.

Her hands traced their way to his waist and she dipped her fingers underneath the band before unbuttoning his fly. He felt each hesitant and shaky movement through the thin fabric of his boxer shorts and his own hands froze on the clasp of her bra.

"If you keep touching me like this," he said, "I'm not going to be able to slow down."

"I don't think I can stop touching you. When you're near me, I seem to throw every bit of common sense out the window."

He understood the feeling all too well.

"Are you sure about this?" He could tell she was nervous and he didn't want her regretting anything afterward.

"I've been waiting a long time to feel like this and there is no way that I could bear it if you stopped now, Cooper."

The second he heard his name on her lips, he was lost.

He had no idea where their clothes went, but within seconds, she was lying naked in the bed, his body stretched out on top of hers. There was nothing between them but hot, smooth skin and a raging determination that quickly moved from a pulsing ache to a desperate need.

She opened her thighs. She was so slick with desire he practically slipped right into her. He pulled back, and she whimpered in protest. He used his hand to stroke her into temporary satisfaction while he fumbled in the nightstand drawer for the box of condoms he'd bought on his last trip to Boise. He hadn't been anticipating things moving this quickly between them—hoping, maybe—but a soldier was prepared for anything.

She was so tight and wet around his finger he almost regretted having to withdraw so that he could roll the contents of the foil packet over himself.

Once he settled back between her legs, she arched up to receive him. He moved slowly at first, kissing her as their bodies joined and learned each other's movements. But as she urged her tongue quicker in his mouth, he thrust his hips to match her speed.

When she cried out, he felt her muscles contract around him, and he poured himself into her—and not just physically. He'd never let go like this before, and he was surprised at how he couldn't wait to let go again.

Chapter Eleven

Just past midnight, after their second round of lovemaking, Maxine collapsed on top of Cooper, her heart pounding, her lips spreading to a slow smile. This time around, they'd gone much slower and had been less frenzied as they'd leisurely explored each other's bodies.

Did she seriously just have sex with the man? Twice? She hadn't lied when she'd said she'd waited a long time to feel the way he'd made her feel. But the more accurate truth was that she'd never experienced that kind of physical sensation and release—even with Bo. As embarrassed as she was about her lack of intimacy, recent or otherwise, Maxine now feared that one night with Cooper had unleashed an uncontrollable passion inside her, and she had no idea how to get her emotions back in check.

It wasn't as if she hadn't thought about a natural progression of dinner leading to lovemaking, but they'd blown right past the set table and straight into the bedroom.

She buried her head against his neck, fearing she'd see regret in his eyes.

He ran his fingers up her spine until they rested along the sides of her head.

She lifted her face, and he kissed her softly, not letting her go.

"I take back what I said earlier about liking your hair."

Her hand flew up to the tousled mess. She'd spent hours trying to tame her curls into place this afternoon and could only imagine the crazy disaster her bird's nest had become. She attempted to finger comb the mess, but judging from the tangles and fullness, she knew it was no use.

He captured both of her wrists into one of his, drawing her hands down to his chest. "What I meant was that it looked beautiful before, but now that I've seen it like this, I don't ever want to see it any other way."

She shook the blond tresses out of her eyes and leaned back. Sitting on top of Cooper like that, straddling him, she felt like a warrior queen who'd just conquered the world.

"And if you promise to leave it all loose and wild," he said, pulling her down and then rolling her over until he was in the power position. "I'll feed you some cold chicken sautéed with mushrooms and artichokes along with a side of overcooked orzo."

"I'll do whatever you say if it means I get a sexy, virile man to cook for me."

"Deal!"

She playfully smacked his bare rear as he hopped off the bed and walked naked to the kitchen. She'd thought his chest had been incredible but it was nothing compared to the sight of him from behind.

She could certainly get used to him—to this.

Stop it, Maxine. One reckless night of passion didn't

mean they were heading straight into the realm of serious relationship. After all, just last week this same man had all but told her he was like a tumbleweed without roots.

She followed him into the kitchen, intent on trying to act as normal as possible. Or at least as normal as a woman who hadn't had sex in a while could act after the passion she'd just unleashed in the bedroom.

They ate a reheated dinner in bed, then fell asleep in each other's arms. After a third session of lovemaking in the morning, they took a shower together.

"So, I need to pick my suit up in Boise today," Cooper said as he pulled on a pair of jeans.

"Okaaaay." Where was he going with this?

"Did you, uh, have to pick up Hunter or anything this morning?"

"No, I'm not supposed to get him until tonight."

"Oh. So you're free all day?"

"You know, if you want to ask me something, Cooper, you can just ask it." She knew what he was trying to suggest, but she didn't want to seem so eager to spend more time together that she'd invite herself along on his errand.

He blew out a breath, and then gave her a sheepish smile. "Sorry. It's a really bad habit I have. My ex-wife once said I was the best investigator she'd ever seen, but that I have the communication skills of a canned ham— great for emergency situations, but sealed up tight with a preserved shelf life that she couldn't wait around for."

Wow. He was finally telling her a little something about himself that she hadn't been able to pick up from letters or Cessy's background check. The fact that he was talking about his ex-wife right after they'd spent the night making love didn't exactly bolster her uncertainty about things progressing so quickly between them. But she'd opened up to him about Bo, and besides, when would she get another shot at learning more about him?

"So is that why you guys got a divorce?" Maxine slipped her clothes from last night back on, trying to make the question sound as neutral as possible in the hopes that Cooper would keep talking.

"That might be the main reason, but really Lindsay and I were never suited for each other in the first place and we lasted only a couple of months before she set her sights on marrying up to the next rank. Last I heard, she was married to a chief warrant officer and now has a couple of kids. Which worked out better for both of us."

Cooper shook his head, pulling on a pair of jeans. "I've always been a loner, which is why I think Gregson paired me up with Hunter as pen pals. When I was twelve, my mom died of a heart attack probably caused by working too many jobs and dealing with too much stress. The day after the funeral, my stepdad decided he didn't want the responsibility that came along with raising a kid so he turned me over to the authorities. I bounced around in the foster care system until I joined the Corps when I was eighteen. You can say I'm preprogrammed to keep my mouth shut and my emotions to myself.

"Anyway, I guess I should have just come out and asked if you wanted to drive down to Boise with me." He grabbed a T-shirt out of the rustic maple dresser and pulled it on over his head as if he was sliding his emotional armor back into place.

She took the hint, knowing that he was effectively shutting down the conversation, just as he had last week when they'd been talking about plants and putting down roots in Sugar Falls. She wanted to respect his boundaries and not push for more information. Nor did she want to say the wrong thing and make him think she was patronizing him with sympathy or pity. A man like him wouldn't respond well to either. So she simply smiled and said, "I'd love to go to Boise. Thanks for asking."

They reverted back to the more comfortable informal banter as they finished getting ready—neither one mentioning the obvious shift in their relationship.

She had yet to ride in the beat-up yellow Jeep, but knew her car would be more suitable for a road trip to the city. He agreed, then grabbed her keys, insisting on driving, and opened the passenger door for her.

"I see the time you spent in the kitchen last night didn't diminish your need to reassume your preferred male-dominated role." She arched a brow, then slid into the car.

"And I see the time you spent begging me for more didn't diminish your need to get off your girl-power kick." He bent and placed a kiss directly on her mouth, effectively cutting off the argument on the tip of her tongue.

As he navigated the road down the mountain, she relaxed and allowed herself to bask in the way it felt to have a man take care of her for a change. She definitely didn't *need* Cooper around, but after years of doing for herself and Hunter, it certainly was an added bonus. Plus, she liked being with him.

It was almost noon by the time they arrived in Boise. She was surprised when he drove past the Towne Square Mall, where Cessy recommended he shop, and instead drove toward the more eclectic shops downtown.

"I'm starved," he said. "You want to grab a little lunch before you help me update my wardrobe?"

"I might need more sustenance than that if we're talking about a complete update."

"Are you saying you don't like my clothes?" He looked down in disbelief at his olive colored T-shirt, and she almost grabbed the steering wheel to keep him from veering toward a one-way street.

"I'm just saying your closet could stand to have something other than jeans and old green shirts that should've been put out to pasture back when you were a corporal."

"Says the woman who wears a daily uniform of sexy denim and white."

"I like white. It's my signature color."

"It makes you look like an angel." He put his hand on her thigh as they stopped at a busy intersection. "A fallen angel."

She shoved him playfully before pulling him right back toward her for another kiss. She enjoyed the way they'd been teasing each other today and wondered if she would have appreciated his sense of humor all along if she hadn't been ready to jump down his throat at every comment he'd made.

They had lunch at a sidewalk café, and she took him to her favorite Western store, talking him into some new footwear.

"You sure I won't look like a tool trying to fit in as a country boy?" he asked as he eyed the handcrafted leather cowboy boots he'd just tried on.

"Positive."

"They're actually pretty comfortable. I'll make you a deal. I'll buy the boots, but you have to let me get Hunter that tent and sleeping bag he wants."

"Is that your way of talking me into letting my son go camping with you?" Geez, the man had a way of phrasing questions that always left her second-guessing what he meant. Why couldn't he just come out and make his intentions known? It was almost as if he didn't want to risk her saying no. Which made sense now that she knew about his childhood. But she thought they'd been moving past that stage.

"If you don't want us to leave you out, you can come along, too." He smiled in invitation, and her tummy flipped at the implication of them doing anything together like a family.

"Hunter can go, but I'm a maybe. It'll depend on whether Jake Marconi goes and I'd have to risk having fish guts flying around. Either way, I don't want you to buy Hunter any camping gear. You don't have a job yet, and I'm not sure what your budget's like…"

"I may not be living in the Cessy Walker lap of luxury," he replied. "But I've never been a big spender and I have a pretty good nest egg saved up. So I can afford anything I need."

And then, to prove it, he bought the boots, as well as something from each store they visited. He spent way more than even Cessy would have, had she been with them, and Maxine had to wonder where the man would put all his purchases if he decided *not* to stay in Sugar Falls.

All week long she'd forbidden herself from thinking about whether or not he would be leaving. Now, after last night, she didn't think she'd be able to stand it if he did.

She was helping him pick out a tie to match his new suit when she finally figured out a way to bring up the dreaded conversation about the chief of police job.

"You know, you probably have that interview wrapped up and in the bag," she said. "You probably could forgo the whole suit-and-tie thing."

"That's what everyone at the Cowgirl Up keeps telling me. But I still want to look my best. I don't do anything half-assed."

"So, if you took the job, when would you start?"

He shrugged. "Probably midsummer. Usually, there

are exemptions and reciprocity agreements for military police transitioning into civilian law enforcement. So if I get hired, I'd still have to attend an abbreviated police academy. But it would just be a short, supplemental-type course to get me up-to-date on laws specific to Idaho."

Wow. He'd already done the research, so it sounded as though he was seriously considering the job. She thought of re-creating more nights like the one they'd just spent together, and she locked her knees together to keep from doing a little happy dance right there in the men's accessories aisle.

He held up a camouflage-colored tie, and she shook her head, unable to wipe the growing grin off her face.

"How about something in a soft pink or pale yellow?" she suggested.

"No way." He wouldn't even look at the two options she'd pointed to. "Those are girl colors."

"Speaking of girl things, I heard there've been a few women who applied for positions with the new Sugar Falls PD, but that whoever they pick as chief would have control over who gets hired."

"Yep, that's what the mayor told me."

"Would you be opposed to working with women if that's who applied for the officer jobs?"

He turned toward her and set down some of his shopping bags before pulling her in for a soft kiss. "I know you think that I'm stuck in the Stone Age about some things, but not about women. I've been in combat with females who are tougher than most of the guys in their unit. I've been on the range with some who could outshoot me. And I've been in interview rooms with female officers who had a criminal giving a full confession while everyone else was standing there scratching their heads."

"That's good to hear."

"Why? Are you thinking of a career change to law enforcement?"

She scooted closer to him, breathing in the smell of his shower gel and remembering all the exact spots he'd rubbed it this morning. Geez, she was a sucker for his dimples.

"Nope. I just wanted to know if I'd be evenly matched if I had to put one of your lady cops on notice for flirting with her new boss."

"Jealous?"

"Let's just say that I don't like to share."

"Well, then let me assure you," he said, kissing her lightly. "Not only am I more than professional and above reproach when it comes to my work, but I also don't like to *be* shared."

She kissed him back, wondering if they'd just committed themselves to something. But apparently, neither one of them was the type to just come right out and say it.

Someone coughed discreetly. "Excuse me."

Cooper pulled back and glared at the shorter salesman who'd dared to interrupt them.

The man tugged at his cuff links, averting his gaze as if the last thing he wanted to do was help some couple who were getting hot and heavy in his sophisticated store. "Can I help you two find something?"

"Yeah, a room," Cooper whispered in her ear, as they turned toward the disapproving sales associate. He kept his hand firmly on her hip, as if he would only concede so much. "I was in here last week and bought a suit," he told the man. "The alterations are supposed to be finished, but I need to get a shirt and tie to go with it."

"Very good, sir. Did you have an idea as far as color goes?"

"Not green," Maxine said. She was rewarded with a

playful pinch that she doubted the snooty clerk would've approved of.

"The suit is dark gray," Cooper said, reverting to his military-like formality. "So something to go with that."

"What's the occasion? Are you looking for something festive or something professional?"

"Professional. It's for a couple of job interviews."

A couple? Maxine's gaze shot to the man who'd all but confirmed that he didn't want any other woman but her, yet Cooper was already following Mr. Snoot.

Her boots clicked quickly on the marble floor until she caught up with them.

"Did you have more than one interview lined up?" she asked, trying to pretend as though she was more interested in the yellow paisley silk tie than the answer that could change her—and her son's—whole life.

"Oh, yeah. I assumed Hunter would have told you. Colonel Filden, my commanding officer, is friends with the assistant director of the NCIS offices in San Francisco. He wanted me to apply there, and I figured it would be good to keep my options open."

Mr. Snoot asked him about neck sizes, leaving Maxine to deal with the unexpected blow while the two men moved on to the tables loaded down with dress shirts.

Her heart raced and she felt light-headed, just as she had when she'd been a cheerleader and had been thrown up in the air to do a basket toss jump the very first time.

And just like then, she'd been flying free one second, then, when her base team had missed the catch, she'd been flat on her back in the middle of the football field the next second. The air had been knocked out of her, and she'd had to command herself to breathe, just as she did now.

Her hands trembled as she steadied herself against the colorful rainbow display of neckwear.

What was with that line about keeping his options open? Was she one of his options?

Sure, they'd agreed to keep things between them simple— no strings attached. So then why was her body reacting as if his leaving would send her into a tailspin?

She thought he'd been actually considering the police chief job, but she should've trusted her gut all along. Cooper was bigger than anything their small town had to offer. Of course he'd be more interested in working for a federal agency in a huge city.

But she'd been so caught up in the initial rush of their new romance that she'd had no idea about the NCIS gig. And while Hunter might have known about it, he'd only considered the one option that meant he didn't have to think of the possibility of losing Cooper.

Heck, after last night, she might've let herself believe that she felt that way, too. But she was a lot older than her son and should've known better.

Maxine had anticipated that Cooper would get tired of Sugar Falls and take off for a bigger city, but couldn't he have mentioned this before last night? Before she completely gave her body and her heart to him?

"What about this one, Max?" Cooper held up a pea-green shirt.

But she was too flustered to rise to the bait. She needed to catch her breath. She needed to get herself together and stop acting like a brokenhearted little girl. She gave him a thumbs-up before heading toward the restroom, where she turned on the faucet. Then turned it off. Then turned it on again.

How had she so completely misread everything? It took her at least ten minutes of pacing the tile floors and deep breaths before she pulled herself together.

This was her own fault, and she promised the woman

looking at her in the mirror, from here on out, she would come up with a plan to extract Cooper from her life. But until she devised one, she had to face the music. She couldn't stay in the bathroom forever.

When she finally met him by the register, he asked, "Are you okay?"

"Just feeling a little off. Must've been what I ate for lunch."

"But we ate the same thing. And I'm feeling fine."

She just bet he was.

He put his receipt in his pocket and picked up several shopping bags and the plastic covered suit.

"I guess some things affect people in different ways," she said, not talking about food. "You, apparently, can handle things better than I can."

"Okaaaay," he said, as they exited the store. But from the drawn-out way he said it, she knew he wasn't convinced that everything was all right. "If you're not feeling great, maybe we should head home."

It's not your home, she wanted to shout at him. But anger equaled passion and she didn't want to feel anything for him anymore. So she just nodded and allowed him to lead her to where they'd parked the car and open the door for her.

While he drove them up the mountain, she kept her eyes closed, hoping he'd think she was feeling too poorly to talk.

He switched on her car radio and set the station to Motown, even though she knew he didn't like her favorite music. But he was doing it for her and she was acting like a petulant child who wasn't being allowed to have her cake and eat it, too.

Over and over her mind replayed what he wanted for

his future and why she and Hunter weren't enough for him. But she'd be damned if she'd bring it up.

"Why don't I take you home?" he asked. "Then I'll pick up Hunter at the Marconi's house."

"No!" She couldn't have her son's classmates and their parents wondering why Cooper was driving her car. "I'm feeling better. I'll drop you off and go get him myself."

She thought he'd be relieved to be off the hook, to not have to play the role of family man. But he frowned at her before pulling his sunglasses out of the center console and shoving them on his face.

They passed the cookie shop, and when he turned off the road toward his cabin, she heard him mumble something about separate cars and wearing disguises. But she was too wrapped up in her own emotions to pay attention to his grumbling.

When he parked the car, he asked, "You sure you're okay?"

"I will be," she said, as she got out of the passenger side and walked over toward the driver's side.

He moved toward her as if he wanted to kiss her goodbye, or at least hug her, but she knew if she let him get close, she might start crying right there in his driveway.

"Don't forget your shopping bags in the back," she told him. The redirection allowed her to slip behind the wheel and put on her seat belt before closing the door.

"So, you want to run tomorrow?"

Yes, she did. In fact, she wanted to run right now. *Away* from him, not with him. "We'll see."

"I mean, if you're feeling better."

"I'm sure I will."

He studied her as if he suspected she might not feel better that soon. And he was right. How long did it take to heal from a broken heart?

Chapter Twelve

To: mcooper@yahoo.net
From: hunterlovestherockies@hotmail.net
Re: My Mom
Date: April 30
Hey Coop,
My mom's been acting kinda sad lately. I've never seen
her so mopey. She won't tell me what's wrong, but maybe
you can talk to her. Your a real good detective. I think
she might be in trouble with the law because I heard her
talking to Aunt Kylie and Aunt Mia about the NCIS office
in San Francisco. Then she said that she shoulda known
better all along and never shoulda let her guard down.
If she goes to jail, can I come live with you?
Hunter

Maxine had been avoiding him for two weeks. Cooper
didn't need to glance up at the calendar tacked up next

to the cabin's refrigerator to know exactly how long it had been. They'd shared the most fabulous night of his life, and she'd made him feel things he hadn't known his canned ham of a heart could feel. When they'd gone shopping afterward, they'd teased each other, they'd laughed at each other's jokes and they'd freely packed on all the public displays of affection they hadn't been able to exhibit in Sugar Falls.

The next thing he knew, she was feeling under the weather and, before she'd even dropped him off, she was back to being the ice angel.

That's what he got for telling her about his past. For wearing his heart on his sleeve.

At first he thought she was legitimately sick and he'd been concerned about her. But when she left him at the cabin, obviously well enough to go pick up her son on her own, he'd assumed she was stressed about talking to Hunter about the shift in their relationship.

Ever since then, he'd suffered through her painful politeness every time he brought Hunter home after practice and a distant coolness every time they saw each other around town. He was desperate to talk to her to find out what had changed and to ask if he'd done something wrong. But he couldn't bring himself to go to her and expose his vulnerability.

She'd made it clear that she didn't want their relationship—whatever it might be—to be known about in town. He could always speak to her in private, but what if she laughed at his neediness? What if she told him she didn't want to be associated with him at all?

They always seemed to beat around the bush with each other and, up until the night they'd made love, he'd been very careful not to put his heart out there. Unfortunately, that night and the day after, he *had* flung his heart out there for her to see—and discard.

Thankfully, he'd done so outside the Sugar Falls gossip mill and didn't have to suffer a public rejection, as well.

This was why he didn't do relationships. When it came to talking about his feelings, he couldn't express himself.

He hadn't even told her that the moment he'd walked in for his interview, Cliff Johnston handed him an employment contract that he'd already drawn up. The Sugar Falls Police Chief position was his, if he wanted it. But how could he take the job when, for all he knew, Maxine was hoping he'd save her the embarrassment by leaving and getting out of their lives?

His first instinct was to do just that. But the problem was, he didn't want to make a decision until he knew exactly what she was thinking and why. And he'd been too damned scared to even ask. Each time he'd come face-to-face with her since their time in Boise, he'd turned back into that lost, abandoned twelve-year-old kid again, with no one to look out for him, no one who cared.

But last night at baseball practice, while the team was in the dugout making fart jokes and seeing who could cram the most bubble gum into their adolescent mouth, Cooper realized he wasn't a little boy anymore.

He was a trained investigator, and a soldier. He made his living seeking out the truth and solving mysteries. What kind of law enforcement officer would he be if he didn't confront Maxine and find out how she felt—even if the answer hurt him?

He sat at the kitchen table, looking at his printed itinerary for his San Francisco flight so that he could meet up with the NCIS Special Agent in Charge. He'd hedged his bets and booked the trip knowing that he wouldn't be able to handle living in Sugar Falls if he couldn't be with Maxine.

Then, this morning, when he checked his inbox and saw the email from Hunter, the pieces of the puzzle began to come together, and a seed of hope began to sprout.

Was it possible that Maxine had been upset at the thought of him taking a new job and moving away? If that was the case, then that *had* to mean she cared about him.

It made sense, now that he thought about it. The last thing they'd been talking about was his interview in San Francisco. Then she'd withdrawn.

Under normal circumstances, Cooper wasn't so slow to connect the dots. But then again, Cooper wasn't good at personal relationships—or at falling in love. But sweet, innocent little Hunter might have unwittingly given him the one clue that would explain Maxine's sudden case of cold shoulder.

His heart picked up speed, and he stretched his arms over his head, trying to ponder the possibilities. He didn't want to get his hopes up, since he knew where being wrong would lead. But he had to know. And there was only one way to find out for sure.

He shoved his feet into his new boots and grabbed the keys to the Jeep. He didn't want to jump right into any accusations or force any confessions without gathering more facts and locking down his case. Plus, he looked at his watch, realizing it was too late to talk to her alone. Her employees would already be at the bakery getting ready to open the shop for the day. If he wanted to confirm his suspicions, he would need to talk to her when nobody else was around. The last thing either of them wanted was an audience.

Ten minutes later, he pulled the Jeep into a parking spot in front of the Cowgirl Up Café. On his way to the entrance of the diner, he gave Klondike and Blossom a pat before going inside. He couldn't believe he was already used to seeing the two horses loitering on Snowflake Boulevard and knew that one of his first duties as police chief would be to regulate the potential traffic hazard.

It was a bit late for the breakfast crowd, but he would have to make the most out of his reconnaissance. He took his regular seat at the counter and waited for Freckles to come around with her pot of coffee.

"So is it official yet?" The busty, older waitress asked, as she filled his mug.

That seemed to be the question of the week since most everyone in town wanted to know if he was the man who was going to head up the new police department.

"I'm trying to work that out," he said, purposely being ambiguous, hoping the woman would be her normally inquisitive and informative self.

"So what's stopping you? Are we too small a town for a city boy like you?"

He nodded toward Scooter and Jonesy. "How could a town full of crazy characters like those two cranky cowboys not keep me on my toes?"

"So then your heart is elsewhere?"

"Nope. I'm pretty sure my heart is right here."

"I figured as much. So then what's the holdup, darlin'?"

"Well, my heart is here. But if I stay here with it, I want to make sure it stays intact."

Freckles clicked her tongue and shook her head. "I thought you were a smart fella'."

Cooper leaned back in his chair and stared at the woman who managed to work in the food service industry every day with three-inch painted fingernails. Did she just call him stupid?

"How do you think you can get through life keeping your heart locked up in a jail cell?" she asked.

"I guess I just figured it would be safer being in solitary confinement."

"Honey, the only thing safer in solitary confinement is perverts and snitches. You need to put your ticker back into the general population."

He chuckled, then took the warm mug between his hands. "How do you know so much about prison life, Freckles?"

"Now that's a story for another day, darlin'. But trust me when I say everyone gets their heart broken. You're not the first, and you won't be the last. Now, how a person recovers from it is what separates the men from the boys. You gotta face the hurt and let it make you stronger. Why do you think I named this place the Cowgirl Up?"

He took a sip of his coffee, pondering her advice. "You definitely are a wise woman, Freckles. And I'll certainly take your suggestion into consideration. I bet you're a pretty good rider, too."

"Who me? Heavens, no. I'm deathly allergic to horses. Can't even get within ten feet of one."

He looked at the pictures and the diner decor, realizing his assumptions had been wrong. Maybe he'd been wrong about Maxine, too.

"Hey, Cessy," the waitress called out.

Cooper turned toward the front door and saw Hunter's grandmother heading his way. Great. She was probably here to pressure him about the job.

"Morning, Freckles," Cessy said to the waitress as she lowered herself on the seat next to Cooper like a royal monarch taking her throne. "I'll take a cup of tea and the fruit and yogurt plate. Hold the pineapple, the melon and the strawberries, and go easy on the yogurt."

"What's left?" he couldn't help but ask.

"Bananas. They're a great source of potassium, Matthew." He didn't correct her use of his first name. Probably because he was starting to get used to the motherly socialite treating him like a child.

"I'll have the chicken fried steak, eggs over easy, biscuits…"

"No, no, no," Cessy interrupted. "You have to get in shape for the academy. You can't be putting on the calories like you used to." She turned to Freckles, "He'll have the fruit plate, as well."

"Sure thing." The waitress abandoned him to deal with the reigning queen bee of Sugar Falls.

He took another sip, and the coffee burned his empty stomach like acid, which would probably be more pleasant than the third degree he was about to get from Cessy Walker.

"So, have you told Maxine yet?" she asked.

"Told her what?" This was a new and interesting line of questioning.

"That you're staying in town and taking the chief job."

"I haven't told anybody because I'm not sure that's what I'm going to do."

"Cooper, let's not waste any more time with this maybe, maybe not business that you and my daughter-in-law engage in. Hunter and I have worked too long and too hard to get you two together for you guys to blow it by refusing to talk to each other. It's time that you put all your cards on the table."

Whoa. That's what he'd planned to do, although it wasn't any of her business.

Wait. What did she mean about her and Hunter working so hard? He didn't know which part of that little speech to address first.

"How do you know what's going on between me and Maxine?" he asked cautiously.

"Look, son, you may think that I'm just a pretty face with a big circle of friends, but I've been around a few years and understand men and women. Besides, it doesn't take a detective to figure out that you and Maxine have got it so bad for each other that neither of you can even look at the other without running out of the room with your tail between your legs."

It was only ten in the morning and already he'd been called stupid, out of shape and a coward.

And by two different women.

"Maybe there's some attraction there," he admitted. "But how would Hunter know that? And what do you mean that the two of you have been working to get us together?"

"If you haven't figured it out by now, Hunter is a lot more astute than most kids his age. Anyway, whose idea do you think it was to get you to come to Sugar Falls?"

"Hunter's?"

"Of course it was Hunter's. And why do you think he wanted you here so badly?"

Cooper shrugged his shoulders. He was at a complete loss. "I figured because we were pen pals and he liked me."

Cessy put her head down into her jeweled hands as she shook it. "Maybe I need to call Mayor Johnston and tell him we picked the wrong man for the job. How are you gonna get those two knuckleheads—" she looked up to nod toward Scooter and Jonesy "—to stop leaving their horse poop all through town if you can't even figure out what's right in front of your face?"

He rubbed his hands along his jeans, trying not to crumple the napkin in his lap. He was about to tell the woman to cool her jets and start speaking English when

Freckles put their orders down on the counter. When he saw his big plate loaded down with meat, eggs, potatoes and gravy, he winked at the waitress.

"Really, Freckles?" his uninvited dining companion asked.

Cooper wondered how many people defied Cessy Walker's wishes and lived to tell about it. But instead of further chastising the café owner, she took the empty plate from Freckles' hand and used her fork to fill it with almost half of his food.

"What are you doing?" Cooper couldn't believe the woman had helped herself to his breakfast and planned to eat it. And Freckles had brought her the extra dish to do so.

"Oh, relax. You can have some of my bananas." She pushed her own plate toward him, and Freckles laughed as she walked back to the kitchen. The waitress sure knew her customers.

Had he known he'd be subjected to insults and food theft, he would've gone straight to Maxine's bakery. But these women were definitely providing him with some valuable insight. If he could only figure out what it was—and whether any of it was accurate.

"So you were telling me about your grandson's master scheme." Cooper curled his arm protectively around the remains of his breakfast.

"Of course Hunter liked you and you two guys clicked, but he also knew you'd be perfect for his mom. I wasn't so sure because that girl can be downright fierce in her independence and women's lib hoopla and all that. But he talked me into speaking to the city council and pushing for a police department. Mind you, I don't go around creating jobs on the whims of a ten-year-old boy. The city really does need it, though. Anyway, I figured if Hunter was right about you, then it'd be a win-win."

"So Hunter gets me here, and you lock me into the position as chief, but then what? You can't make people fall in love. Even you, Cessy Walker, have limits to what you can control."

"True. I wanted Bo to be as in love with his new family as I was. But no matter how much I tried, I couldn't get that boy to settle down and see reason."

"And now you're trying to get me to see reason?" Cooper didn't know if he liked being lumped in the same category as Bo Walker.

"Well, you do seem to be a bit more levelheaded. Bo was never cut out for being a father and husband, not like you are."

Nobody had ever told Cooper he was cut out for family life—including his own family.

"How do you know I'd be good for them?"

"How do you know you wouldn't?"

"I've never been that great at relationships."

"Bull. Just look at you and Hunter. He adores you, and you've been wonderful for him. You guys are like two peas in a pod."

Maybe the woman had a point. He'd had no problem opening up to the kid and letting him get close. And Hunter had taken to him, as well.

"Okay, let's suppose that I stay in Sugar Falls. That doesn't mean that Maxine will agree to a relationship."

"How do you know she won't? Have you asked her?"

That was the thing. He *hadn't* asked her. Yet.

"Just as I thought." She nodded as she finished off the small plate she'd filled with his food before attacking her own. "Son, if you want her, you gotta go after her."

It was a catch-22. He knew that if he exposed his love for her, he'd be risking rejection. His other option would be to just leave and never know what could've been. He'd already decided on the former, but he'd allow the interfering older woman to provide him with more information about what Maxine's answer might be.

"I plan to. But she might say no."

"Then you tell her to change her mind. I love that girl as if she were my own, but she can be just as stubborn and prideful as you seem to be. She says no to me all the time, but that doesn't stop me from doing what's best for her anyway."

No, it certainly didn't stop Cessy.

He wasn't one for pep talks—and certainly not from people like Cessy or Freckles. Still, he couldn't help thinking it was time to cowboy up.

That night, Cessy had just picked up Hunter for dinner when Mia and Kylie knocked on Maxine's apartment door. She'd told her friends earlier in the day that she wasn't up for their usual Thursday night out, which obviously let them know she was in an emotional state of emergency because they showed up anyway, setting several grocery sacks on the counter as soon as they walked into the kitchen.

"Is there anything left in the snack aisle at Duncan's?" Maxine asked, peeking inside at the contents.

"Only the low sodium pretzels and some rice cakes," Kylie said. "We even brought this limited-time bacon and waffle kind that Mia wanted to try. Gross." Kylie scrunched up her nose and tossed the unusual flavor to the dance instructor, but Maxine caught it midair and tore it open, grabbing one to taste.

Mia eyed their friend. "So I'll assume from the way you're moving into the bag that something bad has happened with Cooper?"

Maxine told her friends about the night they'd spent together, leaving out some of the more intimate details, and then about the trip to Boise when he told her he was potentially moving to San Francisco. "I saw his Jeep parked in front of the café this morning, and all day I've been waiting for him to come around and say his final goodbyes."

"Wait, back up," Kylie said. "I know that I'm no love expert, but at any point during your conversation in Boise, or since, did you tell him that you wanted him to stay?"

"Of course not! I've been there, done that. Remember when Bo accused me of interfering with his long-term goals? He acted like I'd gotten pregnant on purpose and then forced him to run right back to his mama in Sugar Falls."

"Honey, you know you can't compare every man to Bo," Mia said absently as she went through the cupboards. "It's not fair to you or to Cooper."

After the way he'd handled Nick the Stalker, Mia thought Cooper should be awarded a medal of honor. She obviously was biased. Still, perhaps she had a point.

Maxine sat down and thought about her recent comparisons and her reactions. In her head, she knew that Bo had unjustly blamed her for his own failures. But in her heart, she'd been so beaten down by his accusations and finger-pointing that she didn't want to put herself in a similar position.

She was too strong a woman to resort to begging a man to stay—and too afraid of being hurt again to stand the thought of being rejected if she did ask.

So these past two weeks, she'd swallowed down the lump in her throat and smiled when she saw Cooper around town, but she couldn't bear much more than a few awkward words. He was leaving. And if the guy wanted to move on, she wasn't going to keep him from following his dream.

* * *

Maxine might not have come up with a concrete plan last night, but Mia and Kylie had talked some sense into her and had definitely made her laugh. She was now awake earlier than usual because she'd been too restless to sleep. She knew she needed to tell Cooper how she felt, even if it meant running him out of their lives forever.

The only thing that gave her any peace of mind was making her dough in the early predawn hours. And at this rate, she'd stockpiled eighteen extra batches and wouldn't have any more room in her freezer if she kept hiding from her problems.

Maybe she should expand her business. Or she should start a program sending cookies overseas to soldiers. That was an idea. With summer vacation around the corner, she and Hunter could travel around to various military bases and pass out cookies. Maybe then her son could find a new pen pal, one who was skinny and pimply and read poetry—and who didn't put her senses on high alert every time the very essence of his masculinity poured into the room.

She heard a booming knock at the back door and was thrilled to have a distraction. At least, until she looked out the peephole and saw the subject of her thoughts with his fist raised, about to start his obnoxious pounding again. She unlatched the dead bolt and threw open the door before his knuckles could make contact again.

"Are you serving a warrant or something?" she asked. "You're going to wake up Hunter with all that racket."

"We need to talk." Cooper looked as if he hadn't slept in days and she wanted to rub her fingers along the crease in his forehead and soothe him.

"Good morning to you, too," she said instead.

"Don't do that." He strode past her and looked up the

stairwell before turning back to her, his hands on his hips as if he was ready to do battle.

"Do what?" She closed the door and returned to her mixing bowl, bracing herself behind the unnecessary, but comforting task.

"Don't sidetrack me with small talk. You've been all polite and distant with me ever since that night, and it's driving me crazy."

"I'm supposed to be sorry for being polite?" What exactly did he want her to say?

"Here's the deal. You know how I told you about my ex-wife and the canned ham?" he asked, but didn't wait for her answer. "Well, that's why I'm not good at relationships or personal conversations. I don't want anyone having access to the little opener key that could unseal the tin around my heart." He leaned over the counter, looking into her eyes. "See, if I let you open me up, then you'd see that I'm just a bunch of processed, pressed pieces of leftover bits that nobody really wanted."

She slammed the bowl against the counter, forgetting about her sleeping son. "How could you possibly think that I wouldn't want you?"

"I don't know! Probably because for whatever reason, you and I can't seem to have a normal conversation without one of us either tiptoeing around or barking at the other. Unless we've got our hands all over each other's bodies, I'm too afraid to ask you direct questions, and you're too reserved to tell me what you want. So let's do it now. Let's throw all our cards on the table."

His nostrils flared slightly, and she suddenly felt a great empathy with every poor soul who'd had to sit across an interrogation table from him.

"Okay," she said. "You go first."

"I'm sure you've heard by now that they offered me the

chief of police position. I haven't accepted yet because I've been waiting for you."

"For me? I thought you were waiting to hear about the NCIS job. You said you wanted to keep your options open."

He ran his hand through his hair, and she stood a little straighter, not willing to back down now that the taboo subject was out there.

"I only lined that up in case I needed a backup plan. Now your turn. How would you feel if I took the job here and didn't move to San Francisco?"

"Are you asking me if I think Hunter and everyone else wants you to stay?"

"No, Maxine, I'm asking you if *you* want me to stay."

"I don't want to force you to do something you might resent me for later. Sugar Falls is a small town, and you're used to a faster pace. What if I tell you that I want you to stay, and then you miss out on a fabulous opportunity in the big city? I don't want to be the one who held you back."

"You know I'm not Bo, right?"

She nodded, her hand trembling on the stainless steel bowl she clenched tightly to her.

"And you know that I can swim in any damn pond I want to swim in, and it doesn't matter what size fish I am, right?"

"Yes. I think. Are we talking about you staying or are we talking about fish?"

He moved toward her and took her shaky hands in his.

"I love Hunter. And I don't want to be just a pen pal to him—I want to be a dad to him. More than that, though, I love *you*. And I don't want to have to pretend to you or anyone else that I don't. I'm telling you right now, if I take the job here, I'm not going to be sneaking around town with you or acting like what we have isn't the most incredible thing that's ever happened to me. And if that's too threatening to your precious reputation, then you're going to have to marry me because I won't stay in Sugar Falls unless I have both you and Hunter full-time in my life."

Maxine's heart was churning faster than the butter machine in the corner. "Did you just *ask* me to marry you or did you tell me to marry you?"

"Well, I sort of asked you, but I really don't want to give you the option of saying no."

Maxine knew just how much the entire revelation had cost him. And if he could lay down his pride for her, then the least she could do was open her own heart to him.

"Honestly? I think I fell a little in love with you before you ever moved here, when I saw all those letters and emails between you and Hunter and realized you were exactly what he needed. And when I saw you in person almost daily I had to fight to keep from falling in love even more. I convinced myself you would only be here for a short time, and when you left, it would bring nothing but heartache—not only for Hunter, but for me, too. So I figured it would be safer to keep my distance.

"I thought I was strong enough to have a physical relationship with you because that would be better than having none of you at all. And, just for the record, I wasn't trying to keep our relationship a secret because I was ashamed of you. It was because I was ashamed of being so weak. As long as nobody found out how I felt about you, then I wouldn't have to suffer in public when you finally said goodbye."

"That's the only reason you didn't want anyone to know?"

"Yes. And when it looked like you were going to move here permanently, I let my defenses down, only to hear you mention the possibility of leaving again. I wanted to be woman enough to keep you, but at the same time, I needed to be woman enough to let you go."

He circled the counter and slipped his arms around her. "I don't want you to ever let me go."

"I won't if you promise to tell me that every day for the rest of our lives." Her eyes filled with tears, and, as a drop spilled out and trickled onto her cheeks, he wiped it away.

Then he flashed those dimples. "Just to be clear, that's a yes? You want to marry me?"

"You better believe it, Chief Heartthrob."

He pulled her closer. "I might need you to make me believe it. Do you think there's enough room for a testosterone-fueled guy like me in your girl-power life?"

He kissed her gently, and she let the wooden spoon she'd been holding clatter to the ground. She deepened his kiss and proved just how much room she had to accommodate him, and that she would never, ever let him go.

Neither of them saw the grinning ten-year-old standing in the stairway, sending out a text message.

Hunter Walker: We did it, Gram. Operation: Dad is a success!!

* * * * *

Don't miss Kylie Chatterson's story,
WAKING UP WED,
the second book in Christy Jeffries's new
Harlequin Special Edition miniseries
SUGAR FALLS, IDAHO.
On sale February 2016, wherever Harlequin books and
ebooks are sold.

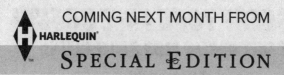
Available January 19, 2016

#2455 FORTUNE'S PERFECT VALENTINE
The Fortunes of Texas: All Fortune's Children • by Stella Bagwell
Computer programmer Vivian Blair believes the secret to a successful marriage is compatibility, while her boss, Wes Robinson, thinks passion's the only ingredient in a romance. When she develops a matchmaking app and challenges him to use it, which one will prove the other right...and find true love?

#2456 DR. FORGET-ME-NOT
Matchmaking Mamas • by Marie Ferrarella
When Dr. Mitchell Stewart begins volunteering at a shelter alongside teacher Melanie McAdams, he falls head-over-stethoscope for the blonde beauty. Once burned in love, Melanie's not looking for forever, even in the capable arms of a man like Mitchell. Can the medic's bedside manner convince Melanie to open her heart to a happy ending?

#2457 A SOLDIER'S PROMISE
Wed in the West • by Karen Templeton
Former soldier Levi Talbot returns to Whispering Pines, New Mexico, to make good on his promise to look after his best friend's family. The last thing he expects is to fall in love with his pal's widow, Valerie Lopez. Now, Levi's in for the battle of his life—one he's determined to win.

#2458 THE DOCTOR'S VALENTINE DARE
Rx for Love • by Cindy Kirk
Dr. Noah Anson's can-do attitude has always met with success, both professionally and personally. But when he runs up against the most stubborn woman in Jackson Hole, Josie Campbell, nothing goes the way he planned. It will take a whole lotta lovin' to win Josie's heart...and that's what he's determined to do!

#2459 WAKING UP WED
Sugar Falls, Idaho • by Christy Jeffries
When old friends Kylie Chatterson and Drew Gregson wake up in Las Vegas with matching wedding bands, all they want to say is "I don't!" But when they're forced to live together and care for Drew's twin nephews, they realize married life might be the happy ending they'd both always dreamed of.

#2460 A VALENTINE FOR THE VETERINARIAN
Paradise Animal Clinic • by Katie Meyer
Single mom and veterinarian Cassie Marshall swore off men for good when her ex walked out on her. But Alex Santiago, new to Paradise and its police department, and his adorable K9 partner melt Cassie's heart. This Valentine's Day, can the doc and the deputy create a forever family?

**YOU CAN FIND MORE INFORMATION ON UPCOMING HARLEQUIN® TITLES,
FREE EXCERPTS AND MORE AT WWW.HARLEQUIN.COM.**

HSECNM0116

REQUEST YOUR FREE BOOKS!

2 FREE NOVELS PLUS 2 FREE GIFTS!

HARLEQUIN®

SPECIAL EDITION

Life, Love & Family

SPECIAL EXCERPT FROM

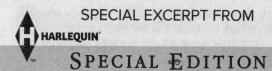 HARLEQUIN®

SPECIAL EDITION

*Dr. Mitchell Stewart experiences unusual symptoms
when he meets beautiful volunteer Melanie McAdams.
His heart's pounding and his pulse is racing...could this
be love? But it'll take some work to show commitment-
shy Melanie he means forever...*

Read on for a sneak preview of
DR. FORGET-ME-NOT, the latest volume in
Marie Ferrarella's
MATCHMAKING MAMAS miniseries.

Closing her eyes for a moment, Melanie sighed. She had
no answer for the taunting voice in her head. No theory
to put forth to satisfy her conscience and this sudden,
unannounced huge wave of guilt that had just washed
over her like a tsunami after a 9.9 earthquake. And, like
it or not, that was what Mitch's kiss had felt like to her,
an earthquake. A great, big, giant earthquake and she
wasn't even sure if the ground beneath her feet hadn't
disappeared altogether, thanks to liquefaction. She felt
just that unsteady.

She'd stayed sitting down even after Mitch had left
the room.

*Damn it, the man kissed you. He didn't perform a
lobotomy on you with his tongue. Get a grip and get back
to work. Life goes on, remember?*

That was just the problem. Life went on. The love
of her life had been taken away ten months ago and for
some reason, life still went on.

Squaring her shoulders, she slid off the makeshift exam table, otherwise known in her mind as the scene of the crime, tested the steadiness of her legs and, once that was established, left the room.

Whether Melanie liked it or not, there was still a lot of work to do, and it wasn't going to get done by itself.

She had almost managed to talk herself into a neutral, rational place as she made her way past the dining hall, which, when Mitch was here, still served as his unofficial waiting room. That was when she heard Mitch call out to her.

"Melanie, I need you."

Everything inside her completely froze.

It was the same outside. It was as if her legs, after working fine all these years, had suddenly forgotten how to move and take her from point A to point B.

She had to have heard him wrong.

The Dr. Mitchell Stewart she had come to know these past few weeks would have never uttered those words to anyone, least of all to her.

And would the Mitchell Stewart you think you know so well have singed off your lips like that?

Don't miss
DR. FORGET-ME-NOT
by USA TODAY *bestselling author Marie Ferrarella,*
available February 2016 wherever
Harlequin® Special Edition books and ebooks are sold.

www.Harlequin.com

THE WORLD IS BETTER WITH

Romance

Harlequin has everything from contemporary, passionate and heartwarming to suspenseful and inspirational stories.

Whatever your mood, we have a romance just for you!

Connect with us to find your next great read, special offers and more.

f /HarlequinBooks

@HarlequinBooks

www.HarlequinBlog.com

www.Harlequin.com/Newsletters

HARLEQUIN

A *Romance* FOR EVERY MOOD™

www.Harlequin.com